STUCK FOREVER

By

Kosisochukwu Onwe

Copyright.@.Kosisochukwu

Onwe

TABLE OF CONTENTS

CHAPTER ONE...........................4

Mamieu-crescent.....................4

CHAPTER TWO......................12

The animal thing....................12

CHAPTER THREE....................19

Weird characters 19

CHAPTER FOUR.....................29

The life changing decision 29

CHAPTER FIVE.........................40

The cloning trial.......................40

CHAPTER SIX 51

Molly's doom..........................51

CHAPTER SEVEN 61

The cat in the bag 61

CHAPTER EIGHT 73

Neutral mother.......................73

CHAPTER NINE 86

The unexpected little friend 86

CHAPTER TEN..........................95

Team MOM 95

CHAPTER ELEVEN....................103

Be calm, I'm here 103

CHAPTER TWELVE..................112

Black...?.................................112

CHAPTER THIRTEEN 121

Spanish challenge 121

CHAPTER FOURTEEN 129

Here comes the queen 129

CHAPTER FIFTHEEN 147

"I heard that".........................147

CHAPTER SIXTHEEN 164

CHAPTER SIXTHEEN 164

Scale of innocence..................164

CHAPTER SEVENTEEN 174

The most unforeseen news 174

CHAPTER EIGHTEEN...............182

Indeed, death isn't an excuse.182

CHAPTER NINETEEN...............190

The miraculous intervention ..190

CHAPTER TWENTY 201

Similarities – Genetic lock up .201

CHAPTER TWENTY ONE 215

The strategic confrontation....215

PROLOGUE

Donald's thesis periodically matured into a clear genetic manipulation. Biological science upgraded to the next level after his death, thereby providing a plus to the global list of biological inventions.

The interval between 2032 to 2046, engulfed multi challenges the Chopkins and Gozax city would have never expected in a century. Although, the new biological invention brought them a win-win declaration, it still took a lot.

CHAPTER ONE

Mamieu-crescent

The weather is cold and cloudy with no signs of constellations in the sky. It seems there will be a rainfall. The natural light has phased out leaving the street lights, fence lights and outside lights to illuminate the streets. Few rooms still have their lights on.

Mamieu-Crescent Street is as clean and lonely as a cave. One could hear the movement of his muscles and joints on this pathway. Mamieu-C is one of the longest streets in Tokex district of Gozax city. It is an open-end avenue, with its start from a T-junction between Tony-Katex mall and Barbie road and ending with Tokex science high school.

Tokex district has its major traffic on the T-junction leading to Mamieu because of Barbie road which covers a significant distance and Tony-Katex mall. The mall has one of the highest sales traffic in the whole of Gozax. From statistics, it ranks second in of about 1to 2.5billion dollars per day.

With this estimate, one can detect the stable and wealthy economy Gozax is endowed with. Nonetheless, the socio-economic status of its citizens can never be the same with all considerations in check. Roadside sellers began to form a chain-like formation close to the fences of houses into Mamieu-Cresent Street to meet the daily demands of people who could afford the high price tags in the mall.

This scenario creates a very busy atmosphere in Mamieu-C Street especially in the late evening hours. The coarse buying and selling noise coming from the street has a great bounce-back effect on the residents making them adapt to it as well as turn into noise sources with time.

Mamieu-C's busy nature also links to six more streets which are attached to it, all bearing the major first name –*Mamieu*- and these are the suffixes attached to it respectively: *Gold*, *Beet*, *Yellow*, *Purple*, *Cara* and *Green*.

The subsidiary streets have its own link to Mamieu-C which was named after Gary Mamieu, the first man to organize a street sanitation outreach in the district.

The aim of the sanitation exercise was to clear the roadside gutters, situate waste bin sites, trim the road side flowers and trees and a simple opportunity to unite people living in Pintoma as the street was formerly called. After each sanitation outreach, he always reaches out to people with incentives like fruits, snacks and drinks, a way of saying "Thank you for coming".

This particular act makes them turn up for subsequent sanitation exercises. With time the other six streets joined the trend to keep their streets and environs clean. After his death, the streets took to his surname *Mamieu*, laying emphasis to their differences with colors. Eleven years after his death, Mamieu's day was inaugurated in his remembrance to bring people together once in a year to celebrate their unity.

These streets have much effect on each other as they share the same schools, hospitals, parks, markets, churches, transport means, play grounds, library and fueling stations.

The daily activities go intertwined in these streets round the clock. This as well has much effect on the daily peaceful nature of Mamieu-C.

Unlike the normal atmosphere, there is no movements, car rushes, high-tone randomly heard voices, pedestrian jams, street music, loud production process machineries, after school rush, road side market tantrums and train horns (Pooh-Pooh) passing through Mamieu to Leach district targeting Gozax as its terminal.

All the noise and commotions seems to have been strangely paused remotely; it is midnight.

All and sundry is static to get some rest and set out for the next day's activities. The cloudy weather brought fort cool breeze that sings swift lullaby into rooms with opened windows and puffs out its curtain to escape in a blink.

Suddenly, there is a strange monotone sound on the mail box outside Mamieu-C 88 residence. Simultaneously, the light to Molly's room went off in response to the strange sound. She quickly closed her laptop slightly. In curiosity, she stood up from her reading table guided by the dim light from her laptop's screen, she tip-toed gently towards her window unknowingly followed.

She knelt close to the window's edge to peep through the curtain, as she pulled the curtain; she saw an unclear shadow in a bent position close to the entry alarm at the gate. As she tried to lean forward carefully close to the windows hinges in order not to be noticed, she felt a close soft tickling touch on her left ankle making her shout out noticeably in fear. Immediately, she closed the curtain to see what touched her, and then her cat meowed looking straight into her eyes. She sighed in relief.

She reached out to touch its neck swiftly when she suddenly heard a familiar voice.

"Who's there?" the voice asked.

At the same time, she quickly pulled up her cat to the window, raised the curtain and they tilted out their heads.

"Mario, is that you?" she asked in a little bit high tone.

Mario is a middle aged man who earns a living through picking up trashed canned drinks from dirt sites and resells it to canning industries.

He dresses dastardly like though he is mentally ill. He walks in a bent position, pushing his head forward as a result of aftermaths of sickness due to aging.

"Yes," He replied as he bent down to pick up something

Still in curiosity, "What are you doing out there, you freaked me out?" she asked.

He slowly stood erect and answered. "I have some soft drink cans to gather."

"At this time? You should be sleeping."

"Only if you will shut down your laptop and save your eyes the stress," He replied harshly turning to leave.

That response hit her badly because Mario was right.

"Please be careful with the mail box next time, at least it's wooden." She retaliated insolently as she closed her curtain.

"How did he know my laptop is on?" She asked herself. Then her cat meowed again. She smiled at it and cuddled it as she walked back to her reading table. She placed the cat on the seat and bent close to her table to continue with what she was doing. "Okay, I'm gonna place the order right here." She thought out loud as she clicked on the bumpy *Click to order* button.

The time on the lower task bar caught her attention as she was closing the site.

"Wow! 3:26 am!" She said out loud.

"Bedtime," she told her cat as she quickly closed the laptop, flung herself to the bed and slept off.

*   *   *

Morning in the Chopkin's residence is often sort of a dizzy one as the children were graduates without jobs. Apparently, there isn't any call for morning rush. But the routine wasn't the same for Susan, so she became their inevitable annoying alarm clock.

"Dear Robin, wake up," Susan said as she opened Robin's door.

"I'm up mom, Good morning."

He replied turning sluggishly to the other side of his bed.

"You are not up Robin," Susan said still standing by the door.

"I am mom, at least my eyes are open," he replied raising his head to confirm he is awake.

"Alright, do get off the bed for the day's activities." She asserted sensibly, as she relieved her body from the door's frame. "I'm sick and tired of waking you both up every morning." She said out loudly as she proceeded quickly to Molly's room.

"Molly is just worse, heavens help me," She said when she opened Molly's door, she beckoned on her angrily, "Molly, will you be responsible for once and get your ass off the bed?" Not getting any response she quickly traced the wall for the light switch with her right hand and switched it on.

"Oh my God!" She screamed in fear with her eyes wide open and her right hand against her chest.

"What is it mom?" Molly asked curiously as she quickly jumped up from her bed.

"Why in heaven's name will you keep this scary thing in your room?" She gestured to the wall.

"Oh mom, you scared me, that's a lion's head mask, there's nothing wrong with it," Molly groaned as she lay back on the bed.

"Molly, it's scary. You should be mindful of these things," She said with concern and sat down on the bed. She stared at her daughter for a while.

"What is it?" Molly asked.

"How are you dear?" Susan asked ignoring her question. When Molly didn't answer, she gently touched her cheeks with a smile on her face.

"I'm fine mom, how was your night?"

Molly is a 23 years old, light-skinned young lady. Her facial structure and expressions always gives a weird outlook that makes her different from everyone else. Her eye balls are bulgy and rolls round freely in its socket like a pinball whenever she wants it to, her eyes are separated by a nasal bone pointing fort her nose which is flanked by her puffed cheek whenever she laughs.

Her dentition looks clustered with little or no gap separating her semi-white teeth from each other. Her laughter always seemed different because her middle two incisors always come out first like that of a rabbit followed by other teethes in a clustered arrangement. Her upper lips push up her nose to contrast the eyes a bit when she laughs giving her a rare look. Her

milk colored hair can be spotted from anywhere. In her fifth grade, she got a part of her hair colored with ink which made her look less ordinary.

Everything about her seems unusual. One wouldn't say she is ugly or beautiful because of her beautiful soul and awkward face. Her less concern and insignificant attention to fashion makes her appear shabby and naive most often.

Although, Margie helps to sharpen her fashion sense, little or no difference is always achieved. It's either she misses her color combinations or the cloth is way bigger than her. "On a very good day you will comfortably wear an unprocessed animal skin as clothes." Margie would often tease.

Molly's love for animals over shadows everything that needs to be looked into in her life. Socially, she is dumb;

financially, she is unstable; spiritually, not recommendable and physically, below the zero line.

The only thing that impresses or entices her is animals. Her love for animals made her go to school and obtained a Bachelor of Science degree certificate in Veterinary medicine at Tokex Science College.

"I'm fine dear," Susan replied looking around Molly's room in amazement.

"Where in God's name do you get all these wild life pictures?" She asked again in curiosity.

Molly looked around at the pictures and then to her mom smiling. "It's very easy mom," she replied as snuggled closer to her cat.

At the sight of Molly's room, one would declare it's an animal's gallery. Close to the door, from the right stands the statue of a giant tiger. Her cat will always mew at every sight of it. The reading table is just at the comfort sight close to the tiger because she always loves caressing its hairs while reading.

Close to her bed stands a head lamp that has animal stickers stamped all over it. Directly over the head of her bed stands a very big parrot statue she named Chokey. Her wardrobe stands close to the lion's mask Susan saw when she stepped into the room.

Every part of the wall has a large album of aquaculture, mammals, wild animals, birds, reptiles and insects all over it and no trace or picture of their family. Her life seemed to be stuffed with animals.

All her actions, vocal signs and behavioral gestures radiate that of animals. She got absorbed into the similarities with animals over time. At the end of each day her conversations are either with Margie, Chokey or the giant tiger. Even though she gets no response from them, she has no one else to talk to.

CHAPTER TWO

The animal thing

Susan stands up, crosses her night wear firmly and moves close to the reading table.

"You know you should get a job," Susan advised as she pulled out the chair and sat down.

"I have a job Mom," Molly replied sitting up. "Douglas still pays me monthly salary," she explained further looking intently at her.

"You mean he gives you peanuts," Robin chipped in standing by the door with crossed arms. He asked that in a mockery tone.

"Robin stop," Susan shunned him. "You know you aren't getting enough from there?" She asked

"I know mom, not like his lab isn't working. It's just lack of huge customers. Besides I love the setting and it's all about my passion," Molly explained.

Susan wasn't sure of words to say, but she needed to clear her point but still lacked words to use. "Hmm," she breathed out hard

"Okay," she said as Robin moved in to sit with Molly on the bed. She gave him a quick angry gaze which prompted him to ask, "What?" But she said nothing.

"You remind me so much of your father, Molly," Susan complimented calmly.

"Yeah," Molly affirmed.

"Because of the animal thing?" Robin asked frowning.

"Yeah the animal thing is there, but the outrageous zeal, strong spirit and determination is just same as hers," She answered as Molly put up a bold smile. That seemed like the most comforting thing she has heard in a while.

"We got married to each other with all the love fantasies intact. We went for vacations, did all that is worth it and took out time to express our love and care for each other. His love for animals never stopped him from loving me more. That lured me into loving animals too. Your birth was the best things that happened to us Robin," She said.

"Not until, he took up the cloning project," She continued.

"You mean animals to humans?" Molly interrupted while trying to sit upright.

"No," She answered, "Animals to animals."

"That's exactly my research project in college, but mine deals with animals to humans which are almost the same thing," Molly said excitedly.

"How did it go mum?" Robin asked.

"Donald made dog hybrids with different animal genes and DNAs. Its success was used for the war over Xylom," Susan replied as she blinked back tears.

"Xylom?" Robin and Molly asked simultaneously.

"You mean the Xylom limestone site?"Molly asked curiously.

"Yes, but we lost to the Boatabs because the hybrids with the carnivorous clones began seeing the herbivorous clones and soldiers as prey and began to hunt and kill them.

Gozax withdrew from the war due to loss of its military personnel and clones, giving in to Boatabs."

"Wow!" Robin exclaimed.

"Donald still continued with the research to close the lapses of the project. Then he decided to capture and tame a lion alive. Subsequently, use the tamed lion's serum as specimen for cloning. His major aim was to provide a safe atmosphere for all the clones," She said as she leaned back on the chair and continued.

"He started the taming process which began yielding some success over time. That was 4 months into your conception Molly. On one of his sessions with the lion, he tried to assess the ability of the lion to detect a friendly face and not harm it. Before this he made pictures of himself and positioned it before the lion but the lion was helpless when he got to it. He decided to practice this in real setting. Donald made the lion chase him," she broke down in tears.

"He fell on the ground lying upwards to enable the lion see and recognize his face; but it didn't get the memo. It launched it claws into Donald's stomach." She closed her eyes as she remembered how it all happened. Molly rushed and hugged her in tears as Robin stood close patting her back in sympathy.

"It's okay mom," Molly said in tears.

Still in tears, "I did all I could to save his life. I rushed him to the hospital; I laid by him begging God each passing day to heal my husband. I spent all I had and all his savings but he died."

"Pull yourself together mom" Robin pleaded with a calm tone

After some time of crying and sympathizing with each other, they got over their emotions and wiped their tears.

"What happened to dad's cloning project?" Molly asked.

"Honestly, I don't know. I didn't bother about that. I was engrossed by his pains for the days he lasted. My husband was of utmost importance to me than the project." She replied

"Hmmm," Molly breathed out.

"I was traumatized by his loss that I found it so hard to cope. At nights I would cry tirelessly. The doctors warned me severally of my rising blood pressure because of my physiological condition, but that was least of my worries. All I wanted was to have my best friend back. Douglas had to get me another job forcefully to pull me back on track and prevent me from losing another life."

"So nobody took up the project? And the government did nothing about it?" Robin asked curiously.

"Yes, nothing happened," She answered as Robin and Molly looked down in disappointment.

Molly quickly held Susan's hands firmly, "Its okay mom, I promise to make you proud and revive your joy someday," Molly pledged

After some time of silence, they heard a heavy knock on the door.

"I will get that," Robin said and left.

Then Susan drew her chair closer to Molly and held her hands.

"Molly?" She called sternly.

"Yes mom," Molly answered.

"I was damn serious about you getting a well-paying job." Then she paused for some seconds and continued, "I was fired yesterday."

"What? What happened? Why?" Molly asked in confusion.

"You ask too many questions," Susan replied with a smile.

"I want to know, talk to me." Susan remained silent.

Robin called out from the sitting room.

"Molly, you've got a package!"

"Yes!" She shouted joyfully and rushed out of the room. Susan followed her.

"Please sign here," the delivery man said pointing to the space for signatures.

He handed over her package to her, they bid goodbye and she shot the door.

"What's that?" Susan asked coming down the stairs.

"Of course, I can't order an article not to talk of text book on anatomy of carnivores," Robin replied nonchalantly as he focused on the tea he was making.

"You can be exceedingly annoying," Molly told him aggressively and headed for the fridge. "You should take it easy on your little sister," Susan whispered to Robin.

"Like she deserves it?" He replied carelessly as he headed back to the sitting room.

Five weeks later, in the early hours of Wednesday. People are already moving out scarcely for their various daily activities. The street is not yet crowded; the atmosphere is still cold with less noise. The street lights are still on, buses and cars can be numbered. The bus stops are less crowded and the light to bring fort the day is still dimming its way through. Appreciable voices are beginning to be heard in different residences as families are getting ready to set out for the day's activities.

Suddenly, the St. Felix Catholic Church's large bell began to ring. The bell is one the time setters in Tokex. It is situated in a very high tower; this makes it easier for the wind to carry its sound far and wide.

It goes off at every hour except in midnights; in the morning at 5am it rings to awaken its congregation for the morning mass; unknowingly it as well wakes so many inhabitants of Tokex. On this day, this same bell woke Molly up as usual.

Molly's room is located directly opposite the fence leading to the gate which makes her see and hear what happens at the gate and beyond before everyone else in the house. She sat up on her bed and leaned towards the wall holding Chokey firmly. For a while, she is lost in thought. She clung to her pillow tightly as she worried about her mom. She thought of quitting her job at Douglas's laboratory but all she knew how to do was veterinary.

"Nobody likes or appreciates me before now despite my efforts. It will also be the same dejection if I get another job. It makes no sense." She thought.

She sat up when she heard a noise at the gate. Immediately, she rushed to the window to see who it was.

"Robin," she said in amazement.

She couldn't comprehend where he would be going to at that time dressed in a sweater and cap. He looked strange. She moved back to her table and turned on her bulb.

"5:54 am," she said looking towards the window still wondering where he is going. It was definitely not work. She shrugged her thoughts away.

"Not like he cares anyway," she uttered reluctantly as she left the room. She looked so untidy in her disheveled hair and her unwashed oily face made her less attractive. Her oversized night wear made her look bigger than she is.

As she walked sluggishly down the stairs one would think she is mentally ill, but she is in her right state of mind but without less cognizance of her personal outlook. She was making breakfast when her mom came into the kitchen.

"Good morning mom," she greeted.

"Good morning dear," Susan replied. She patted her back as she walked to the fridge.

"Mom," Molly called out hazily.

CHAPTER THREE

Weird characters

"Robin, where did you get this money?" Susan shouted uncontrollably.

"It's none of your business!" He shouted back. She slapped him twice for shouting back at her and he turned away holding his left cheek with his right hand. Then it dawned on Susan that she missed it somewhere in their upbringing.

"Molly makes things easier for me than you do Robin," she lamented in a high tone. At this time, Molly overheard her name and thought Susan asked her to make fried eggs for her, so she proceeded to do that.

"Now it's all about Molly right?" Robin asked angrily.

"Yes, it's all about her Robin," she replied, "Despite her silly behavior, she still gives me peace of mind than you do.

Molly wouldn't earn this amount of money and not hesitate to tell me where it's coming from." She added

"Oh now you worry about the source of my money mom?" Robin asked as he opened the door to walk out and Susan followed him quickly.

"Where are you going Robin?" She asked, "Where are you going to I asked," she questioned as she pulled him back. As Molly poured in the eggs into the frying pan, she heard Susan and Robin raising voices at each other. Then she rushed out to know what's going on.

"I'm leaving your miserable presence mom," he shouted as he turned and rushed down the stairs. Susan rushed to the door before him and locked it. Now Molly could hear them clearly.

"You are going nowhere Robin," she said as she sat down in the sofa holding onto the door key angrily.

"Mom, what's wrong?" Molly asked curiously.

"Your brother rubs banks and stores, the money is in his room!" she exclaimed.

"Robin, what's the matter, what money is mom talking about?" Molly asked calmly.

"Oh! Shut the fuck up," he shouted at Molly and turned away still fuming in anger.

"Mom, Robin bought some foodstuffs for the house," Molly said to lighten the situation at hand.

"What foodstuffs?" Susan asked. Then she looked at Robin. "Robin get yourself into that kitchen right now and take those foodstuffs out of my house before I get back." Susan said angrily and left the house.

Molly tried to walk away calmly but wanted to talk to

Robin as he headed back to his room.

"You know; I think you should give mom some peace of mind. Tell her how you got the money and she will let you be," she advised.

"Molly, mom lost her job, what am I supposed to do?" He turned and replied compassionately.

"I know about that but telling her the source of the money wouldn't make you less human," Molly replied wisely.

Then he shook his head and said, "I've got no explanation for anyone," and headed back to his room.

"Oh! Really?" She said and followed him, "You know your attitude can be hazardous to mom's health right?" She asked as she followed him into his room.

"So now I've got the attitude?" He asked angrily.

"Yes Robin, you should be mom's fortress and not some sort of..." She tried to clear her point but he interrupted her immediately.

"Please spare me those blames, you have suddenly forgotten how I carry most of the responsibilities here, handle the bills and all that I do?"

"Maybe that's not enough, you don't care about how one feels towards your silly attitudes. You pull up stunts like everyone should deal with the dusts you raise. It's not just about paying bills and carrying responsibilities but showing how much you care," she replied in a slapdash fashion with her arms crossed underneath her breasts.

"Really!" He said with raised of amazement.

"Yeah," she replied with confidence with her arms still crossed underneath her breast.

"I see," he concluded raising his eyebrows.

While they were lost in arguments, Margie came into the house unannounced but got choked by smoke all over the place.

"What's going on here?" She asked coughing out loud. Then she noticed it was coming from the kitchen.

"Ah!" She shouted at the sight of fire on the gas cooker. She quickly stretched her hand to the fire extinguisher on the right side of the wall covering her mouth and nose with the other hand and put off the fire. She still coughed as she left the kitchen and staggered her way through the stairs.

"Oh God, I can barely see," she said, "Who's here?" She asked still coughing as she opened Robin's door.

"You think you are worth it with your weird character and looks huh?" Robin asked angrily.

"Yes I am, Robin," Molly replied meanly.

"Can you guys stop this," Margie shouted but was ignored.

"Interesting," he said laughing, "So tell me why mom still doesn't regard you as anything openly? Tell me why you have no friends since you care so much?"

"Robin stop!" Margie warned but was ignored the second time.

"Tell me why dad has to die four months into your conception Molly," he asked meanly. "Everything you come in contact with goes wrong, why?" He added impudently.

"You see Robin, no matter how awful you try to portray me, you can never be better than I am," Molly said in a low tone as she turned and walked away in disappointment.

"You are wrong about her," Margie said and left as well.

Molly rushed out of the house in tears. Margie tried to catch up with her and calm her down.

"It's ok Molly," Margie said.

Molly ignored her and walked straight to Douglas's lab where she worked to cry out her eyes. When she got there, she narrated all that happened to him, he felt bad and tried to console her.

"You know he is right," she said sniffing, "I am disastrous," she said as tears rushed down her cheeks heavily.

"You are not my dear, you are amazing Molly," he said looking intently at her. "If anyone will be proud of whom you are today its Donald. Wipe your tears and do not let this

get to you," Douglas advised. "Always know I will be there for you," he assured her.

"Same here dear," Margie added as she hugged her tightly, "please wipe your tears." She said smiling. Molly listened to them and wiped her tears.

"I really want to make my dad proud, even if nobody appreciates me," she avowed confidently.

"Be strong dear," Margie chipped in while rubbing her back.

Then she continued, "I want to take up dad's cloning project but…"

"But what?" Douglas asked curiously.

"Mom said she doesn't know what happened to the project after his death," she replied.

"That's not true," Douglas said strongly.

"What?" she asked amidst confusion.

"Picasso, Donald's friend took up the project in the memory of your father. But because the government lost interest in the project he left Gozax for Losuzy city to earn a living and probably continue with the project over there. And Susan knows about it." He explained. Molly seemed lost for a while.

"Why will mom hide this away from me?" she wondered.

"I don't know," he replied innocently.

"How do I get anything about the project to start with and consequently search for Picasso?" She questioned amidst perplexity.

"Maybe you should check out his library," Margie advised reasonably.

"I think that will help," Douglas agreed in conclusion.

While Molly went home from Douglas's lab, she had a whole lot situated in her mind. Feelings of emotions, sadness, fear and optimism, encompassed her mind. What if she makes mistakes in the cloning project which could cost lives and lead to failure? Would she leave the family in search of Picasso and quit her job? She is lost in experience of mixed feelings considering family and social factors that could be affected.

"I will take up my college research on cloning," she concluded fervidly.

During her research in school, she chose to carry out a research on human cloning with animals for military advantage. She explored the relevance of her research to the benefits of copying the strength, speed, agility, and strong perseverance of animals to elevate the unique qualities of soldiers during war.

The somatic infusion of animal genes into humans is intended to transform and improve the physical and physiological qualities and performance of soldiers at war. Molly's cloning approach took another dimension to tackle the challenge of reproductive implantation and time.

She assessed the pitfalls of several cloning approaches such as reproductive and therapeutic. Through proper analysis she devised a means to overcome such lapses which makes her research unique. She devised her means by collecting the somatic cells of different in one specimen tube.

Animals she used includes: tamed lion for its perseverance and fierceness, tamed tiger for its strength, hare for its fastness and speed and also squirrel for its agility.

Prominent cloning experts will fertilize eggs and semen of the cloning subjects and await its maturity after so many years before it is being utilized; but through her research she devised a means to avoid that by hypothetically proposing to inject human with animal somatic cells.

Somatic cells are all other cells in the body make up except the egg and sperm cells. They contain forty-six individual chromosomes, organized into twenty-three pairs of chromosomes. There are about two hundred and twenty types of the somatic cells in the body.

Often, they are used in the body to refer to the cells of the body in contrast to the reproductive cells. Molly used them extensively to bridge the gap between timely utilization of clones and successful cloning. She proposes that the easiest way to clone is to extract the somatic fluids of the particular sites of interest and inject it into humans or the subjects to be cloned.

Particularly to this research, she used the somatic fluids of a lion's heart and brain, a tiger's muscles, a hare's brain and bones and the squirrel's brain and eyes. The only challenge she has is unavailability of humans to test the hypothesis on.

As she wandered in her thoughts; she suddenly realized she has walked a far distance so she decided to continue with a bus. She trekked a bit to the next bus stop -*Jolly bus stop*- at Mamieu-Cara Street.

Interestingly, she is always fund of this bus stop because of the big laughing face placed on the roof of the bus stop with *be happy* inscribed underneath its jaw. Each time she steps into the bus stop, she looks up and put up a bold smile too.

Some passengers alighted from the bus and she entered. When she entered she noticed some familiar faces at the end of the bus giggling at her. From the look on their faces she understood they were taking their time to level insults at her.

With this, she didn't border sitting at the end as usual. She gently took off her back bag and sat on the extreme seat on the fifth roll of the bus.

Looking out through the window while in a bus is what she indulges in always. She picks inspirations from people who are consciously going about their daily activities. As the bus moved, she caught sight of two ladies discussing, laughing and walking freely on the pedestrian avenue. One is taller, bigger and more beautiful than the other. At the same time, she remembered Margie and smiled.

Margie is one of the persons she couldn't trade for anything in her life. Margie is a twenty-eight year-old lady and married for two years. At times, Molly would wonder why she stooped so low to her level.

Fortunately, she is the only one that understands and defends her whenever things go wrong. Overtime, Margie turned out to be her only source of consolation, motivation, advice and any support she needed. Her sense of humor makes her stand out amongst all.

They were the only teenagers in high school when they met. Everyone despised her but Margie didn't and that kept their friendship till date. Still in the bus Molly recalled their first meeting. On that day, Molly lost her transport fare back home from school. She did all she could to convince someone to pay for her transport but all to no avail.

"You mean, you used it for chops?" One of them mocked her laughing.

As the time was getting late she decided to enter one of the buses and pled with the driver to pardon her when she gets to her destination. Unfortunately, the driver turned out to be the same with the all others that refused her plea. Then Margie emerged.

"Its okay sir, stop treating her like that." Margie quarreled.

"Will you pay?" The driver asked rudely with his hand outstretched asking for his money.

"Yes I will," she answered as she brought out the money and gave to him. Molly thanked her for that kind gesture.

"I'm Margie," she introduced herself.

"It's my pleasure to meet you Margie, I am Molly," Molly replied while managing to smile.

"Mm mm, the Ms..." Margie said and they laughed. Molly

quickly jumped down from the bus as it started moving and waved at Margie.

"Come to sixth grade, class C during lunch break tomorrow!" Margie shouted from the window. "Okay," she replied.

"Byeee," Margie said and sat back in her seat.

Ever since then, she has been her life saver. Despite their age disparities, they are still best friends.

"Hmmm," Molly breathed out as she realized the bus has gotten to her stop site. She paid the driver, alighted from the bus and headed home. While she walked, she brought out her phone from her trouser pocket and began to type.

"You are still the best no matter what, thanks for being there even when I least expect you to be. B-Mol will always remain grateful for all you do for her. Thanks for everything Margie."

She pushed her phone back into her pocket as she tried to open the door of her house.

CHAPTER FOUR

The life changing decision

She entered and saw her mom seated in the sitting room, watching a television program tuned up to its highest volume.

"Mom!" She shouted. Susan turned quickly.

"Oh," she replied as she picked up the remote to reduce the volume.

"Why make it so loud?" Molly asked.

"I have a lot going through my mind, I needed it to be loud enough to distract me a bit," she explained. "How was your day?"

"Fine," Molly answered reluctantly as she turned to make her way to her room, but turned back immediately when she remembered all that Doulas told her.

"Mom, why did you lie to me about dad's project?" she asked meanly.

"I don't understand," Susan replied in confusion.

"Douglas told me Picasso took over dad's cloning project after his death. Is that true?" She asked aggressively this time.

"Yes," Susan replied incongruously.

"Interesting, so why did you lie to us about it?" She asked again. Then Susan quickly stood up in anger.

"Because I wouldn't want to lose any of you to it too," she shouted, paused for a while as Molly stood still staring at her. "Losing my husband to that deadly project is the most devastating thing that ever happened to me. I wouldn't want to experience such again." She concluded in a low tune.

"Really?" Molly asked curiously. "Dad was victimized out of circumstances not that the research is deadly. That same research was once of good use to this city, remember?"

"I don't care about how good it was, all I know is that none of my children will embark on that again, never." She yelled spitefully and sat down angrily. Molly stood still staring at her for a while

"Fine," she said and headed to her room.

Later that evening, the Chopkins' residence is so desolate. Robin came back and walked straight to his room not minding if anyone was at home. Molly as well locked up herself in her room with the company of Chokey and other of her animal exhibits. Susan felt lonely in her room, so she came out but saw nobody. When she realized the retreat was as a result of the day's incidence, she tried to approach them.

"Robin, come let's prepare dinner together please?" she pleaded standing closely to Robin's door which she usually opens without knocking.

"I'm not interested," he replied in his baritone voice.

"Okay," she said and walked towards Molly's room slowly. As she got to her door, she said calmly, "Molly, I ordered pizza, your favorite flavor, would you mind to join?"

"No thanks," she replied.

Susan did all she could but they wouldn't give in. Then she retired to her bed for the night.

Time rode from weeks into months; the Chopkins were never the same. They went about their various daily activities not uttering a word to each other. Susan tried to get the family back together but it proved abortive. At some point, she called them for a brief meeting.

"I know you are both mad at me; but still remember I am your mother. I may have failed you in so many ways, but I will stand up against all odds to make you both happy." She said

"Including having an affair with Eric, your boss for money? Without our consent?" Robin asked harshly.

"I don't know what you are talking about," Susan replied.

"Tell me this is not true," Molly said frowning.

"I don't know what he is talking about," she shouted with a shaking voice.

"Hahahaha," Robin laughed as he stood up and left.

"Cool" I will be in my room," Molly said and left as well.

Susan bent over her knees and cried bitterly. She couldn't comprehend why they turned against her.

"I miss you Donald," she lamented in tears as she leaned back on the sofa. She fell asleep for some minutes but woke up when her phone rang.

"Yeah, Prisca," she answered in a coarse voice.

"Suzzy, are you okay?" Prisca asked with concern.

Prisca is Susan's colleague at work that she is close with.

"Not really," she replied rubbing her forehead

"Would you mind sharing with me?" Prisca requested in an ally manner.

"Robin thinks I'm having an affair with Eric," she replied nervously.

"Wow, that's huge!" Prisca said and continued, "Did you try to convince him that you are not doing such thing?"

"Yes but Molly seems to believe him," Susan replied coolly.

"Too bad," she said in disappointment, "Suzzy, you will be fine, I'm sure they will come around." Prisca uncertainly assured over the phone.

"Ok, thanks," she replied and hurriedly hung up the call. "Hmmm," she sighed in relief as she rested her head back on the sofa.

In the evening of the same day, Robin suddenly barged into Molly's room while she was reading. She turned quickly in fear and asked curiously, "Are you okay? What's the problem?"

"Relax, I've come in peace," he replied serenely and made his way to her table.

"Okay," Molly replied still wondering why he barged in like that.

"So, I will go straight to the point," he said as he sat. "I'm here to be the big bro you ever wanted." He added with a truce-like smile.

"I don't understand," she seemed confused.

"Relax and let me finish Molly," he said still smiling, "I want to be part of your success story. Molly, I guess I have missed us all this while. I have really stirred up a whole lot in a while now," he asserted apologetically.

"Yes you have," Molly replied crossing her arms underneath her breast.

"Yeah and that's why I'm here to make it up to you. Molly, I'm sorry for all I said to you the last time. Please forgive me, to prove how sorry I am I want to be the human subject in your cloning research," he said sincerely

"What?" Molly shouted and felt his temperature to be sure he is alright.

"What? I am serious Mo…" he replied smiling boldly.

"No you are not," Molly interrupted, "You cannot do that," she added in disenchantment.

"I can, in fact I will. I have deliberated on it and my mind is made up. So far I will come out alive, I will do it for you, Molly let's give dad a name, he deserves it," he said convincingly.

"Really?" Molly replied amidst tears.

"Yeah," Robin assured confidently

"Oh my God this is the best thing that will ever happen to me," she said and hugged him tightly. "You are the best

Robin," she added with gladness.

"Yeah, anything for you," he replied as they let go of each other. "I'm going to tell mom right away," she said and tried to rush out.

"No, don't do that," Robin said pulling her back.

"Why?" Molly asked her smile fading away.

"She wouldn't let us," he replied sadly,

"That's true," Molly confirmed. "The only way we can achieve this is to keep it away from her." He advised

"Ok thank you once again," she said and hugged him again.

"You are welcome anytime dear," he replied and kissed her forehead.

"Come to think of what you said about mom, is it true?" She asked. Then he smiled and sat back on the table.

"Yes of course, I mean I can't lie against her," he affirmed.

"How do you know? Did you see them together in a compromising position?" she queried.

"Chill," he replied smiling as he flung his ear piece's wire across his neck. "My friends saw them," he added convincingly

"Really, your friends can misinterpret their relationship you know," Molly asserted with a bit of distrust.

"I don't know about that. But come to think of it, how did she manage to send us to the best schools in town, carter for us for such a longtime single-handedly. Even now that she got fired I believe it's definitely for a reason." Robin explained.

"Don't make up such things in your mind about mom. It is possible to carry such responsibilities without dad."

"It's alright, if you choose not to believe me, its fine."

"Yeah; anyways, thanks a lot. I will quickly tell Douglas and Margie," she said joyfully with an overwhelming smile

"Alright, remember it's a secret." Robin said as he stood up to leave.

"Yeah."

As Robin left, she quickly jumped on her bed in jubilation. "Yes, yes, yes. Chokey we made it!" She acclaimed with squeezed hands of victory.

With such much joy she jumped down from her bed, quickly grabbed her phone and dialed Margie's number.

"Margie pick up, pickup," she murmured as she placed the phone on her left ear. Suddenly, the phone beeped.

"Hey, you called and waited for me to pick up; sorry, I'm not available please drop a message."

"Margie I called to share the best thing that ever happened to me, don't border to call back, Robin volunteered to be the human subject for my cloning research," she said happily.

"Meet me at Douglas's lab tomorrow morning before work. Bye." She added and hung up the call still smiling..

She sighed in relief and happily as she fell backwardly into her bed.

The night seemed longer than normal to Molly. Her propounded joy couldn't let her get some sleep. The mind has a way of ruminating over memories and imaginations. It occupies the body system with unconscious state of thoughts; it can also make one exhibit involuntarily in accordance to whatever he or she is thinking about.

The mind has the capability of twisting impossible events to be possible. It manipulates the thoughts into imagining things real or unreal. The state of mind changes one's mood to suite itself. The mind can position events from templates of the past, memories or future plans.

In time of love it positions pain or passion, in time of plans it portrays the merits and consequent flops, in lost it shows pains, in the time of failure it positions depression or frustration and in the time of achievements it portrays joy and sense of fulfillment.

The latter is Molly's state of mind and mood, a whole lot ran through her mind: the recognition, her father's name, the joy of final accomplishment, the worth of monetary investment by the government and above all she would be reckoned with something good for once.

Nonetheless, she also thought of whom to name the cloning method after.

"Me? No Robin is there," she thought and shook her head sideways in disagreement. "Dad? What about mom?" She murmured almost silently with no obvious movements on her lips.

"Hmmm," she breathed out heavily, "I will decide that after the cloning trial," she concluded smiling.

Then she stretched out her hand to her phone on the table to check the time, but was marveled.

"1:20 am!" She shouted, "Oh God," she said frowning.

She quickly stood up in annoyance and entered her toilet to pee. When she came out, she grabbed her ever awake cat and stood close to the window. As she pushed the curtain to the left she imagined how happy her Douglas would be when she reveals the news to him.

Douglas could be regarded as the bread winner of the Chopkins. His past relationship with Donald was transferred to his family after Donald's death. People gossiped that Douglas and Susan were having an affair due to how close he is with the family.

Overtime, he played the role of a father to the Chopkins. While still tender, Molly referred to him as Dad, but Robin changed that in due time. Regardless, she still bestows that respect on him. Individually, they will always run to him to lay their complaints and adhere to his advice. Molly never bordered to hunt for job elsewhere other than his Veterinary laboratory because of how sure she was of his acceptance.

Although, his lab isn't bringing much money into his pocket he is contented with what he has.

His integrity and honesty won over Molly's trust over the years. His lonely life is never a challenge to him. One can say he lives like a lay-monk.

His activities encircled in four places: his house, the church, his lab and shopping mall. Hardly will Douglas be seen in any other place asides the above mentioned places.

His religious consciousness is so obvious that it can be detected from his behavior, lifestyle and outfit. His religious attachment makes him look unapproachable but fortunately, he is one of Molly's comfort zones. His humility, high sense of humor and ability to give makes people stick around him most often.

"As such smokers are liable to die young, so are drunks liable to have a worthless life," he will always advice Robin.

With time he got used to the side comments he gets because of his dressing. Children already named him The Rosary Man because he always carries it carefully wherever he goes. Most of his time is spent in the church, at some point; Molly was prompted to curiously ask, "What exactly is your prayer intention in your consecutive church appearances?"

"Well, nothing much," he answered raising his shoulder, "Just a well spent life," he said smiling.

"Just that? I doubt," Molly replied. She probably said that because she saw nothing enticing enough to be good about his life.

For some minutes, she was lost in thought of the great impacts Douglas has made in her life. Then she turned back to check the time again. It says 1:48am; she dropped the phone on the table angrily and laid down her bed.

The night crawled its way into the morning.

"Finally, its morning," she said when she woke up.

She quickly took her bath, dressed up and almost forgot to brush her teeth. She rushed down the stairs, greeted her mom and rushed out immediately. Susan was baffled at the way she dashed out of the house which is unlike her.

"What could be wrong?" She asked herself.

Douglas was already at his lab when Molly got there. She quickly dropped her bag on one of the shelves and rushed into his office happily.

"Guess what?" She asked as she sat on the client's seat.

"I guess that's a good morning," Douglas asked.

"Sorry, good morning," she apologized as Margie also rushed into the office.

"Yeah baby," she shouted as she hugged Molly tightly almost neglecting Douglas's presence. "You needed to see my dancing sessions to the good news," she said with so much joy.

"I can imagine." Molly replied smiling.

"Congratulations dear," she said hugging her again.

"What's going on here?" Douglas asked curiously.

"Oh, my bad, good morning," Margie greeted sparklingly.

"Robin volunteered to be my cloning human subject," Molly told him cheerfully.

"No, Robin can't do that," he replied in doubts as he leaned back on his seat.

"I thought of that too, how is it possible?" Margie asked strangely.

"I don't know, I was disturbed at first when he told me about it, but it's for real," she replied with a bold smile.

"Interesting," Margie said.

"Does Susan know about this?" Douglas asked.

"Well, Robin and I decided not to tell her because she won't allow it."

"I see, do tell Robin I would love to see him."

"You sound so unhappy," Margie quickly asked on noticing his frostiness.

"Yeah, and strange, is anything the matter?" Molly also asked.

"No, I'm cool," he replied managing to smile.

"Well, I will be off to work. Do have fun dear, congratulations." Margie said leaving.

"Thanks dear," Molly replied happily.

"I'm so happy," she said turning to Douglas. After some

seconds of silence, Douglas spoke up.

"Don't you think it's quite abnormal to use your brother as the human subject?" He asked raising his eyes to align with hers.

"No," she replied, "It's just a trial."

"Alright, I will call him right away," he said as he took his phone to call Robin.

"I will rush out to get the medical team ready," she said, "You know it will be done here right?" "Okay," he agreed.

"Thanks," she said and rushed out.

CHAPTER FIVE

The cloning trial

Few hours later, Robin came to Douglas's lab. Douglas welcomed him into his office. After exchange of pleasantries, "You sent for me," Robin said as he pulled out the seat directly opposite Douglas.

"Yes," Douglas replied sitting up. He placed his hands on his table. "Molly told me about your decision with regards to her research."

"Yes," Robin replied, "Is anything the matter?"

"Not really, I'm only worried you decided not to tell your mom," Douglas queried.

"Yes, Mom won't let it happen," he said, "See, I'm doing this for dear Molly and dad, please let it be the only good thing I will do for her."

"Ok, I'm sure you know what you are getting yourself into because anything can happen," Douglas warned.

"Now you are scaring the shit out of me," Robin said leaning back on his seat.

"I only want you to dispose your mind for it," he tried to calm him down.

"Come on it's just a trial, or am I gonna get stuck as an animal?" He questioned sketchily.

"No," he said, "It's fine if you want to pull through with it."

"Cool," Robin said and stood up to leave, "Please keep it away from mom, don't tell her no matter what."

"Okay."

In the evening, Molly put a call through to Douglas informing him of the outcome of the meeting she had with the medical team she contracted.

"The doctor demanded to see Robin for some biochemical tests and as well assess his medical fitness for the trial. He also asked of the family medical consent and approval signatories, I told him I will endorse that. I suppose he will see a dietitian and physiotherapist too," she reported.

"Okay." Douglas replied.

"I told Robin already, I think he has an appointment with the doctor tomorrow," she said.

"Alright," Douglas replied slowly.

"You seem cold about this, are you okay?" She asked worriedly.

"No, I'm fine; the lab will be ready anytime. When is it going to be?"

"In three weeks' time," she answered.

"Cool."

"Bye," she said and hung up the call.

A week later, Susan went to see Douglas. She is worried about Molly's strange happiness and her sudden alliance with Robin. She asked Douglas if Molly mentioned her source of happiness or if he knows what they are up to, but he denied having knowledge of anything they have in plans.

On the speculated day, Robin and Molly left very early to the lab. The doctors, dietitian and physiotherapist had monitored him for the past three weeks to ascertain his fitness.

Molly and the veterinary doctors played their parts well to ensure the extracted somatic fluids aren't contaminated; they also checked the appropriate dosage for him and made sure they have every factor pertaining to the cloning trail under control.

Molly and Robin signed on the family's medical consent and approval form. Douglas signed as the surety. As they stepped out of the room, one of the personnel handed over the theatre cloth to Robin.

"Please, wear this," she said as she handed it over to him.

"Okay," he replied and collected it.

"I will be here," Molly said as Robin went to change.

In a short while, he came back dressed in the cloth which is a bit too big for him.

"I look so weird on this," he laughed while looking at himself on the mirror.

"Yeah," Molly affirmed, "Your hands are shaking."

"Yeah, maybe I'm tensed, but I will be fine," he assured.

"Okay," Molly smiled.

Immediately, Doctor Larry in

charge of the medical team walked up to them.

"Hi," he said.

"Hi," they replied simultaneously.

"Yeah, how are you feeling Robin?" He asked.

"I'm fine," Robin affirmed.

"That's good, from your laboratory test results conducted this morning, it shows you are fit for the cloning trail," he said smiling.

"Alright," Robin replied.

"I will be in the theatre," he said and left. Then Molly turned to Robin.

"Thanks for doing this for me," Molly said.

"It's okay," he replied rubbing her hand.

"Yeah, I will be back," she said.

"Okay," he replied as Molly stepped out.

Molly went to make sure Douglas was at home with what they were about to do, he confirmed he was comfortable since it's just a trial. When she returned she couldn't find Robin. After some minutes, he came out of the toilet.

"We are ready," Doctor Larry announced.

"Thank You Robin, I will be waiting for you right here," Molly said.

"Why do you sound and act like I'm going to die?" Robin asked, "Come here," he said and dragged her closer. "Relax, I will be fine. I love you so much sis," he said and kissed her forehead.

"I love you too," she replied as they hugged each other.

"Good luck," Douglas said and patted his back.

"Yeah," he smiled as he moved into the theater.

Molly, Douglas and a technician (Douglas's staff) were separated from the theater by a transparent glass that enabled them see and hear all that was happening. Inside the theater is Robin, a nurse, anesthetist, veterinary doctor and Doctor Larry. The medical team stood close to the bed Robin laid on in a circular form all ready to start. Then the technician switched on the theater's camera to capture all that will happen.

The theater is illuminated by white lights that can enable one see the tiniest thing the eyes can capture. Medical instruments to be used are all situated in their respective positions.

"Good morning everyone, today we are here to carry out a cloning trial proposed by Molly Chopkins on Robin Chopkins. It involves injecting the somatic fluid gotten from proposed animals into Robin,

then we will watch and monitor his reactions to it for military advantage," then he pursed and picked up the nurse's report.

"Your vital signs assessment this morning suits a normal condition for this trail. Blood pressure 120/86mmHg, blood sugar 98mg/dl, pulse rate 88 beats per minute, not pale, not anemic, no signs of malnutrition, no fractures and internal bleeding. With this, I medically predict we are safe to start,," he addressed them and turned to put on his gloves and glasses.

"Now, before we commence. I would like to ask, Robin, how do you feel? What do you have to tell us all present here?" Larry asked.

"I thank everyone present here, the medical team, Mr. Douglas and my lovely sister Molly. I decided to embark on this to appreciate Molly's efforts and revive my father's lost name. I hereby dedicate this cloning trail to my dad, Donald Chopkins. I also appreciate my mom for everything she has done for me and Molly since our father's demise. I was a bit scared but right now I'm cool," he said laughing. "So, let's do this, to prove the cloning method is worth it and go home."

Molly's smiles during Robin's speech depicted a clear sign of self-fulfillment, love and satisfaction. She felt indebted to Robin for his willingness to be part of her research. As Robin concluded she decided never to neglect family for his action.

"Alright," Larry said. "We appreciate you too," he added.

"Please check all instruments and make sure they are ready for use," Larry said to the nurse. She checked, "Ready," she replied.

"Now we will start, ready?" He asked looking at Robin.

"Yes."

"Good," Larry nodded. "Ready?" He also asked the other medical practitioners.

"Ready," they chorused.

Then the technician switched on a popular classical music, *I do it for love* by Laurel Clarion. The music played in a stereo and is heard through speakers in the theater and outside where Molly and Douglas stood. The classical is to calm down nerves and tension already in air. And also, predict a successful trial.

"Today, 26th of July 2032. At exactly 9:50 am, this cloning trial started," Larry announced audibly and reached out for his hand gloves

Then the nurse felt Robin's pulse rate and pulled his eyes upward. "Pulse rate normal, patient is conscious," the nurse reported.

"Good," Larry commented signaling a start.

"In the right state of mind I inject 0.5ml Anes-370, anesthesia to last for 2 minutes," the anesthetist said and injected it into Robin.

The anesthesia is used to relieve pain and anxiety during the operation. At that point Robin was conscious of all that is happening, but felt no pain in any way as they continued.

"With already checked dosage, I inject 3mls of combined somatic fluids of a tamed lion, tamed tiger, dog, hare, and squirrel for cloning," the veterinary doctor declared and administered the injection. Immediately, they covered Robin with a thick theater cloth and passed him through high ultra sound to see the physiological interactions.

"Every metabolic reaction needed will commence in 30 seconds of injection, he will be out in a minute," Larry declared.

They watched a screen as each fluid moved to their specific sites and started interacting with its similar cells immediately.

"Wow!" Molly said in amazement. In a minute, they pulled him out.

"Are you okay?" Larry asked as the nurse pulled off the cloth and they looked at him keenly to observe any obvious change.

"Yes," he replied with a smile.

For a while, they stared at him confused because of no immediate changes. Then they all stepped back when he grabbed the bed sheet.

"Robin, are you okay?" Larry asked quietly still watching him closely.

"Yes, I just tried to adjust my hands," he replied.

"That's fastness," the veterinary doctor observed and noted.

"His eyes," the anesthetist called their attention, pointing to his eyes.

"Yeah, my eyes move faster than normal, every damn thing is distinct and clear." Robin confirmed joyfully.

"Good, please note that down," Larry told the veterinary doctor as he checked his temperature. "Now, how do you feel?"

"I feel okay, but not perfect as normal. Something changed, my strength, I think I can confidently pull a trailer right now," he joked. "I can perceive the mildest thing ever unlike before."

While he explained he made involuntary gestures and movements which were beyond his control. The veterinary doctor took note of all these.

"Now, Robin I want you to control your mind and brain. Tell yourself what you want to do," the veterinary doctor instructed.

"What exactly?" Robin asked.

"Maybe, I want to become a dog," he speculated.

"Okay," Robin said. In seconds, right under their supervision Robin turned into a dog slowly.

"Wow!" Larry acclaimed. Molly couldn't hold back her tears as she covered her mouth with her hands.

"This is marvelous," Douglas said with his eyes wide open as Robin barked.

"This is impossible," the nurse stated with uncontrolled amazement.

"Good, Robin if you can hear me please turn back to human," the veterinary doctor instructed and slowly he turned back to human breathing a bit harder.

"How do you feel?" Larry asked.

"I feel good," he replied with a bold smile. Then Larry put up his thumb to Molly smiling. Immediately, she hugged Douglas tightly in tears saying, "Mission accomplished."

At this point a new scientific innovation is birthed. A clearly improved cloning method is envisaged. Not only a cloning method but one with a biological, technological, time, and cost advantage.

For a while they are carried away, as they asked Robin of what to do which is within the research outcomes and he did it. At some point, the nurse looked at the electronic sphygmomanometer and frowned.

"Doctor, his blood pressure…" she said and shifted quickly to the sphygmomanometer "It's increasing at a high rate," she noticed.

"What!" Larry asked mildly in shock. He rushed to Robin and called on him, "Robin!"

Immediately, Robin changed to himself breathing harder, with sweats rushing furiously from his skull down to his face and chest

"What's wrong?" Molly asked amidst confusion and fear as she tried to rush into the theater.

"Wait, they will handle it," Douglas said pulling her back.

"I'm losing it," Robin shouted amidst fear breathing harder and faster, this time he kept pulling himself up and down and the veterinary doctor and anesthetist rushed to his side to hold him still.

"Calm down, Robin and talk to me," Larry said.

"My head is banging," Robin said pushing his head backward to raise his neck and tilt his throat up, "I'm losing my mind, please help me," he pleaded now in tears.

"Relax Robin, I'm here with you," Larry assured. He glanced at the demarcation where he knew Molly was and frowned. This wasn't supposed to happen.

There is tension in the theater as everyone is trying their best to keep Robin in check. Doctor Larry is lost in confusion of what went wrong, while he tried to calm him down. The nurse rushed round to get injections ready in case he becomes unconscious.

Douglas and Molly are restless as they couldn't define what's going on. Molly began praying which she has never done in her life. The classical is still playing but now harder with rough bits and sounds sequel to the present situation in the theater.

With time Robin began calming down slowly, but was losing consciousness. His eyes began dilating and closing helplessly.

"No!" Molly screamed, speedily rushed into the theater and held his hand, "Robin!" She called out in a high tone. "Please stay with me," she cried hysterically.

"Ma, please step aside," the anesthetist asked pulling Molly to his back.

At this point, Robin is unconscious, "Robin can you hear me?" Larry asked but got no reply. "Let's administer a CPR," he instructed authoritatively. The veterinary doctor quickly took his position and began pressing hard against Robin's chest with his hands.

"Please get the heat system ready," Larry said to the anesthetist. Amidst the chaos in the theater the nurse passed all the injections she prepared to Larry in a rush and he injected them.

"6, 7, 8, 9, 10…" the veterinary doctor murmured as he pressed against Robin's chest hardly.

"Come on, come on, come on," Larry uttered looking intently at Robin. His intent gazes wished Robin could just wink at him as a sign of life in him.

"Heat ready, 60 degrees," the anesthetist announced as he dragged the two electric iron-like devices he had and pressed it on Robin's chest. The shock pulled Robin up when he pressed it on him. Then the nurse felt the vein close to his

neck and declared audibly, "No pulse."

Now Molly cried even harder while Douglas had his hands at the back of his head in confusion.

"We go again," Larry stated now with unprecedented sweat all over his face.

At the end of the second CPR section, the nurse still affirmed strongly, "No pulse". His consciousness was almost dropping to coma when he sneezed to everyone's surprise.

"Robin!" Molly called out loudly as she rushed to him and held him, "Please stay with me," she pleaded in tears.

"I'm sorry, I don't know what is happening," he weakly said as his eyes closed again.

"No! Robin, do not do this please!" Molly shouted in fear and tears. Her body was trembling now.

Larry and his team restarted the CPR again, but it seemed not to be working. They did all they could but all to no avail. The veterinary doctor kept on pressing his chest to revive him but there was no sign of life.

"Come on Robin," he said while he pressed harder on his chest. Then, the nurse busted into tears. Larry stopped the CPR after so many attempts, carried out all death assessment and stood still. At the same time everyone became gloomy.

"What's going on?" Molly shouted in astounding confusion but got no reply.

Just then, the classical stopped playing.

CHAPTER SIX

Molly's doom
What next???

The classical seemed to have separated them from the actual feelings of what is happening. Until it stopped playing, then they felt the magnitude of what is going on. Even though Larry has all medical proof of lifeless situation, he still doubted his own professional ability.

"This happened too fast, no sign of physiological stress during the trial, where did we get it wrong?" He questioned himself as he leaned down and placed his two hands on the bed Robin is lying on.

He kept staring at the body helplessly without the effrontery to make any medical declaration. The nurse leaned against the transparent glass, with her arms crossed underneath her breasts. Her reddened eyes and face is as a result of her sectional cries since Robin closed his eyes the second time.

Molly cried helplessly and bitterly on Robin's chest, she already knew he has passed on. His body temperature is cooler than that of a fish. She felt no respiratory movements. She confirmed it even when Larry has not declared it.

Presently, she cried for two reasons. Firstly, Robin's continuous statement, "You sound like I'm going to die?" She cried uncontrollably because they all planned and hoped for a quick trial "Let's prove the research is worth it and go home," Robin's utterances kept occurring in her mind like a mix tape.

Secondly, she thought of what to report to her mom. This particularly made her blame herself for not convincing Robin to tell Susan about it. She realized how foolish and selfish she had been and regretted even more.

While lying on his chest, she wished she could turn back the tick-tock hands of time, but three weeks is such a huge time with numerous activities to be reversed. "This is meant to be a trial," she regretted in tears, hitting his elbow simultaneously.

As a daughter, she already knew what her mother was capable of especially when disappointed or betrayed, not to talk of when Robin's state right now is a result of her own foolishness.

Molly remembered how she tried so hard to reconcile with them but instead they formed their own team against her. She already knew Susan's decision concerning Robin's case would be brutal. This made her blame herself and cry the more.

As she cried unceasingly, the veterinary doctor and the anesthetist stood stranded, looking gloomy in response to the situation on ground. As Douglas couldn't wait outside any longer he dashed into the theater to clear his confusion.

"Doctor, what's going on?" He asked.

Then Larry stood erect and removed his glasses. "I'm sorry we lost him, we tried all we could to revive him, but it didn't yield any result. All body physiological states were under check, where the trial went wrong…" Larry was explaining.

"Shit!" Douglas exclaimed regrettably, as he bent his face and placed his two hands on his waist. He didn't care to hear all that Larry had to say to complete his sentence, he already comprehended Larry doesn't know how it went wrong before he could finish his sentence.

"I'm sorry," Larry concluded sadly.

Douglas looked up to Robin and recalled his last conversation with him in his office, three weeks ago. He blamed himself too as he stepped out of the theater weakly and slowly. As human, if it was possible to cry, he would comfortably do it. He got to the transparent glass and looked up to Robin again, shook his head and turned away. He couldn't believe it. One could conclude he is not feeling the situation, but deep down his being, he is pained.

He cursed the trait of love for animals which Molly inherited from Donald. He regretted this cloning research that took his friend's and Robin's life. He felt less of a father as he is supposed to be.

As he ruminated over all this, he also thought of how to face Susan. This is a woman he has seen in a traumatized state before. The fact that he helped her heal from her emotional trauma weakened him.

He remembered vividly of how she came begging to know what her children were up to. But he denied having knowledge of it. Robin's death made him regret not telling her. He kept wandering in blames and regrets when the anesthetist spoke up.

"Doctor Larry, I think we are waiting for too long,"

"Yeah, we should call an ambulance to take him to the morgue," the veterinary doctor affirmed.

"Yeah, do it right away" Larry said to the anesthetist as the nurse began parking her medical bag.

"I will order for the commencement of an autopsy when he gets to the hospital," Larry added as he turned to Molly.

"Molly," he called tapping her shoulder, "You have to pull yourself together, this isn't your fault," he said as she cried harder. "You have to let go," he advised.

"No," she asserted raising her reddened face with cheeks full of paths of tears.

"You have to my dear, get off him and let's do the needful please," Larry pleaded.

After some minutes of begging, she slowly kissed his forehead and stood up from the bed. Larry covered him with the theater cloth as tears rushed down her cheeks heavily.

"Yeah!   Mamieu-Cara. Residence 6b," the anesthetist directed over the phone.

Molly slowly walked out of the theater in tears. Douglas's unrest prior to the trial came to her mind when she glanced over to where he stood. She is so ashamed to face Douglas, so she didn't border to go close to him. Surprisingly, he came to her and held her shoulder.

She turned to face him in surprise and pain. She couldn't still hold back her tears as she bent her face. Douglas lacked the right words to say. All he could do was give her a napkin to wipe her tears. "It's okay, Molly," he said and she quickly threw her arms around his waist and hugged him tightly.

"It's entirely my fault!" She uttered to.

"No, it's not my dear," he replied pulling away so he could look at her face.

"You have no hand in this trial's outcome," he added holding her elbows and looked straight into her eyes. "All we should think of is how to relay this to Susan, your mother," he concluded.

"That's my greatest fear right now," she cried.

"It's okay," Douglas replied hugging her again.

"I can't believe Robin is dead," she murmured in tears as they carried his corpse out of the theater.

"Pull yourself together my dear," Douglas said consoling her.

Larry is the last to step out of the theater. He walked up to them.

"I'm deeply sorry for your loss," he sympathized. "We did all we could, I will place a call for the autopsy immediately, which will be out in twenty-four hours," he concluded as they nodded in affirmation.

"Pull yourself together Molly," he said, patted her shoulder and left. "Take care," he said.

"Yeah, thank you," Douglas replied.

Molly's hanging breath, depicted how lost she is. Then Molly realized her phone has been ringing for a long time.

"Please let me take this, its Margie" she excused herself.

"Sure," Douglas accepted

"Hi," Molly, how are you doing? How is Robin? How is the trial going?" Margie asked joyfully. Her multiple questions came almost at the same time leaving Molly stranded of which to answer first. All she could do is spill the unforeseen.

"Robin is dead," Molly said with a shaking voice.

"What?" Margie screamed, "How?"

"What's wrong?" Charles, Margie's husband asked in the background.

"Robin is dead," she replied in a low tune.

"What? How?" he inquired hastily in shock.

"I don't know," Margie and Molly replied simultaneously but Margie in a lower tune.

"I just can't comprehend it," Molly continued in unquenchable tears "how it happened. It was going well, all of a sudden his blood pressure…" she explained as she bursts into tears.

"Listen to me Molly," Margie said as she tried to wear her deep-pink colored polo, "Stop crying, I will be with you in no time."

"Okay," Molly managed to reply in tears.

"Where are you right now?" Margie asked with a tensed voice as she quickly grabbed her purse on the table.

"Douglas's lab," she answered weakly.

"Okay, stay put I'm coming," Margie said and hurriedly hung up the call.

"Babe, I'm coming with you," Charles said.

"Okay," she agreed as she sat on the bed waiting for Charles to get dressed, "Robin can't be dead," she uttered regrettably covering her face with her hands.

They quickly drove to Douglas's lab and got there in a few minutes. Molly has Margie's shoulder to cry bitterly on without ceasing. After so much detailing of how it happened, crying and consolation. Molly wiped her tears helplessly. They relaxed in the lab until late in the evening when Douglas checked his time. It was 8:26pm.

"We have to take you home Molly," he said.

"Home?" She asked surprisingly, "I can't go

home," she added. Earlier on, she worried the weather was getting darker.

"You have to go home Molly," Charles advised. "That's the only thing to do, you can't keep this away from your mom."

"He is right Molly," Douglas said.

"Yeah, he is right. How do you intend to face her because I'm pretty sure she confronted you on this?" Margie asked Douglas.

He bent down his face because she is right. She is equally to be blamed because he passed a note of warning about keeping it away from Susan but they wouldn't listen. Instead, of retaliating, he swallowed the blame maturely.

"I will handle that when I get there," he looked at Molly, "Let's go."

As they drove home in Charles's car, she thought randomly of what Susan's reaction would be. In spite of all she graded her reaction to be, she still knew it wouldn't be nice.

She quickly remembered when Robin taught her how to resist a Dog's chase when they were younger and tears dripped down her jaw.

When they got home, they found Susan hosting Prisca.

"Oh, I'm glad to have you all here!" Susan said happily as she hugged them one after the other.

"Thank you," they chorused.

"Molly, please come and help me serve them," Susan requested kindly

"Okay," she murmured as she stood up giving Douglas a side gaze.

"Where is Robin?" Susan asked worriedly as they walked into the kitchen. Molly instantly lost guard of herself. She couldn't control her shivering hands which made the wooden ladle she was holding to fall. "Sorry," she said bending down to pick it up slowly.

"Uhmm, I don't know, he should be on his way back," she managed to lie in fear as she stood erect.

"Alright, are you okay?" Susan asked again looking intently at her.

"Yes, I'm fine," Molly replied plastering a smile on her face.

"Okay," Susan said as she turned to dish the food. They went back out to the dining area with the plates.

"Charles and Margie, trust me I won't entertain you in my house if you don't come along with a baby on your next visit," Susan jokingly warned as Molly placed the plates in front of everyone. Prisca laughed out loud.

"We are working on that," Charles replied.

"Yeah, yeah. That was what you told me the last time," Susan said as Molly sat down to eat.

"Come on, give the couple a break Susan," Prisca said and reached out for her glass of water.

"I have been begging for a long time now," Susan replied as they laughed

"Asides that, motherhood is the most fulfilling experience ever," Prisca asserted as the others looked at her to clear her point. Then she continued,

"It takes an overwhelming pain to deliver a child, think of the joy when you carry him or her in your arms?" She added smiling. "Watching them grow can be stressful and time demanding especially for the mothers. But… the greatest joy of a mother is her child's success," she explained further as the others mopped at her absent mindedly.

"So, Margie and Charles whenever you are ready to go into parenthood, please do. I say whenever you are ready because one has to be prepared intellectually and matured enough with sense of responsibility to carry it," Prisca concluded.

"Thanks," Margie said.

"You are welcome dear," she replied as she took another sip of her water.

"I still remember vividly of when I delivered Robin," Susan said smiling.

At the mention of Robin's name, their moods changed except Prisca who kept smiling at Susan. "That must be epic?" Prisca asked as Charles and Margie conversed in low tones.

"Don't you think this food is poisoned?" Charles murmured into Margie's right ear.

"No, stop it," Margie cautioned.

"I'm worried, why is she nice?" Charles muttered again.

"I don't know," Margie replied.

"Is everything alright?" Susan asked them sharply.

"Yes," Charles replied on their behalf.

"Is the food too spicy?" She asked again.

"No, it's delicious," Margie replied.

"Okay, as I was saying," Susan continued, "I wouldn't say it was epic but Donald pulled up a show on that day," she said as she laughed out loud.

"We are listening," Prisca said smiling.

"On that day, Robin didn't take so much time to come out," With this discussion, Molly started having stomach rumbles. She wasn't comfortable any longer. Her facial expression changed, but Susan and Prisca were so absorbed in their discussion that they didn't notice.

"Robin was so tiny, and I prayed he doesn't slip from the nurse's hands as she wrapped him in his small sized blanket," she continued.

"Can you just stop talking about Robin," Molly thought to herself.

"Hey, relax," Douglas cautioned looking at Molly who is sitting right beside him.

"He was too cute," Susan added.

"I can see that," Prisca confirmed as she looked up to see little Robin's picture frames that is hanging close to the sitting room's bulb.

"When Donald came, he carried him on his head and went round the hospital."

"What?" Prisca shouted with her eyes wide open before bursting into laughter. Susan laughed too.

"That's an experience I can never forget," Susan concluded still laughing.

"Yeah," Prisca agreed.

Few minutes into eating and chatting, Susan turned her attention to Douglas, "I saw an ambulance in front of your lab today," Prisca said as she pushed her spoon full of baked beans into her mouth. "Did anything happen?"

Then Molly coughed out loudly to everyone's notice

"Take some water dear," Susan advised as Molly took a glass of water and emptied it into her mouth.

"Sorry my dear," Prisca said as Molly nodded putting up a strange eye contact with Douglas.

"Yes, there was an ambulance," he replied to their surprise.

"Honestly, when I saw it I wondered if animals needed emergency too," Prisca said and laughed.

Right now, the eating pace for the other three slowed down drastically as they are scared of what Douglas's next response would be.

"I think Douglas's dogs now need ambulance to get to the mortuary," Susan teased.

"Not my dogs, Susan," Douglas replied abruptly. Molly could hear her heart beating in her chest.

"Then what is it?" Susan asked curiously as she chewed her food.

CHAPTER SEVEN

The cat in the bag

Susan anxiousness to know what an ambulance will be doing at Douglas's lab made her focus an inquisitive gaze on him. If it isn't animals, then what is it?

Unfortunately, Susan is asking for the wrong devastating answer from the right person. Then Douglas realizes that certain words or statements can really be heavy to pronounce. Throughout his education and experience in life as a full grown man he was never taught of "heavy sounds" or "heavy statements", but this moment, Robin's death taught him a big lesson even with his gray hairs.

For a moment, he sat frozen like an iced fish looking at Susan not knowing the right way to construct his answer. Amidst his confusion, Susan feels she is waiting too long for her answer then called his attention to it.

"I'm waiting," Susan said smiling mischievously as she expects Douglas to say nothing but dogs.

"Yeah," Douglas replied sluggishly as he blinked his eyes voluntarily to buy himself sometime.

Prisca's desire to enjoy her food diverted her mind a bit from the discussion, but still has full awareness of what is going on.

Charles expects Douglas not to hide the truth because that is what he advised Molly to do. On the contrary, he expects the other because the consequence can be fatal. Margie, holds on to her plate tightly with her left fist, with her head bowed low in expectation. She keeps turning a particular portion of rice at the extreme side of her plate reluctantly, to avoid any curious eye contact.

Molly keeps muttering to Douglas almost inaudibly

"Please don't, please don't…" Her plate of food she quietly kept on her laps gave her the opportunity to lower her head too.

Her spoon and plate keeps shaking involuntary because her palms couldn't stop too. Droplets of sweat ran slowly from her skull, through the back of her ear bone down underneath her jaw.

Her breath came faster and noticeable when Douglas slowly dropped his plate of food almost at the edge of the center table. Then, she hopelessly closed her eyes as Douglas pushed the plate forward in order not to fall off.

"Susan?" He called, "Robin is dead." He uttered in a low tune as he folded his hands in between his separated legs, supporting his elbow joint with his knee and bowed his head a bit.

Immediately, the joyful atmosphere ceased. Molly as well dropped her plate of food on the table and sluggishly leaned back on the sofa and tears majestically walked down from her corneas.

"What!" Prisca shouted in amazement of what she just heard.

"No, you must be joking," Susan said smiling forcefully as she brought down her legs which she placed on the sofa she sat on right angled to her left lap. Obviously, she thinks Douglas is joking or pulling a prank. But, she is yet to realize how true it is.

"I'm damn serious Susan," he replied as Susan dropped her plate on the floor still wondering how possible it is. To her it seems like a drama being played on a stage which will in no time turn out to be unreal. She turned her neck slightly to the left and placed her hands on top of the arms of the single seating sofa she sat on, trying to comprehend how possible it is that her son is dead.

"Molly, is this true?" Prisca asked again with her eyes

widely open, sparkling with confusion.

"Yes," she Molly replied as tears rushed down her cheeks heavily. Margie and Charles became anxious of what her reaction would be as Douglas has succeeded in telling her the truth.

"He passed on this afternoon in my lab," Douglas said.

"How?" Prisca asked curiously.

Douglas breathed out heavily. Although, he found it hard to reveal Robin's death to Susan, he still faced another difficulty trying to tell her the cause of his death.

If Robin died in a car accident or a street fight it would be easier to report but cloning, that's unbearable

He summoned courage the second time to say what actually happened because that will ignite Susan's rage the more.

"He submitted himself as the human subject for Molly's cloning trial," he managed to say regrettably as he bowed his head again.

This time, Susan felt it harder and waves of shock ran through her as realization dawned on her. Cloning since her years in marriage has always been bad luck to her, and now it has claimed her son too? Tears fell from her eyes as she turned to look at Molly.

"Cloning again?" Prisca asked as she rushed to Susan's side.

"The trial was going successfully," he continued. "Until his blood pressure spiked up and led to his death. The medical team did all they could but they couldn't revive him."

Susan closed her eyes as tears continued to flow down through her cheeks. Her reaction wasn't what they expected. They were convinced she would be shocked beyond control, wail, shout, hit Molly and possibly slap Douglas. But, she didn't. It would be better if she did but she didn't. Rather, she kept lamenting and crying in silence without much sniffing and voice raising as Prisca consoled her.

This is what the recent happiness and joyful mood is all about right?" She finally spoke up to Molly.

"I'm sorry mom," Molly pleaded crying out heavily.

Susan sighed out loudly in grief as she tries to control herself. "Douglas, you knew about this and decided not tell me…" she paused as she couldn't hold back her tears. "Even when I asked?"

"I'm deeply sorry Susan," Douglas pleaded shamefully.

"I know why you all kept this away from me…" she wiped her right eye with her right hand and continued, "because you all know I won't let it happen," she said and sniffed. "Now, this cloning has cost me both my husband and son, and here I was, celebrating my son's death unknowingly," she added crying bitterly.

"Be strong Susan," Prisca consoled bracing up her shoulder gently.

All this while, Molly hoped for Robin to walk in and announce he is alive and not dead, but her wishes are far beyond possible grant. They all listened to Susan calmly, wearing gloomy faces and their heads bowed low.

"I knew what I was avoiding and here it struck me the second time," she asserted as she cleaned her eyes with her palms to everyone's surprise.

"May God accept his soul, I'm sure he did this for a good course. Let's get ready for his burial arrangements," she concluded. She stood up immediately with a swollen face, took her phone she kept on the side stool and left the room.

"Take it easy on yourself Susan," Prisca sympathized.

For a moment, they all felt a bit relieved for her calm reaction. Now, they raised their heads. Molly gently wiped her tears on each eye with the left and right sides of her right and left palms respectively, as there is hope of surviving Susan's rage. She could feel pains in the lower part of her eyes due to outrageous tons of tears she has dispensed for the day.

Showing a sign of relief, she placed her hands on her laps to align with her knee, breaths in, to push her chest up, laid back her neck on the sofa in a relaxed mood and breaths out. She closed her eyes to remedy the pains she felt.

Margie adjusted to her left to lay her head on Charles's shoulder for comfort as Charles held her left wrist.

"Which mortuary was he taken to?" Prisca asked as Susan walked past her, heading to the stairs.

"Tokex General Hospital," Douglas answered in a relaxed

tune and continued. "They already commenced an autopsy on him which will be out tomorrow evening," Douglas added

Suddenly, Susan stopped on the stairs as if something had pinched her. Douglas stared at her. The others didn't notice the change in movement because of their sitting positions. Molly and Prisca sat on a better position to notice it, but Prisca was focused on getting Douglas's answer by looking at him intently while Molly had her eyes closed.

Margie and Charles had no chance to see Susan's movements at all because their sitting position was backing the stairs. Douglas worried what could have stopped her when she turned furiously and spoke up as Margie and Charles turned at the same time to hear her.

"To hell with the autopsy! To all that have a hand in the so called cloning trial that led to Robin's death, prepare yourselves to rot in prison, because I will pin you all down with everything in me no matter what it takes and who is involved," she roared, breathing hard in anger as Molly quickly opened her eyes in shock.

"I promise," she added meanly, pointing furiously at everyone before she continued walking up the stairs.

For some seconds, her words kept bouncing back to their ears like an echo. Molly kept staring at her in shock as she disappeared into the corridor. Margie and Charles could not believe she said that as they stared at each other in confusion for a while. Douglas slowly rubbed his forehead hopelessly as he leaned into the sofa. Prisca has never heard Susan sound that horrific but she is fully aware Susan meant all she said.

"Wow!" Prisca acclaimed. "I'm short of words," she added shaking her head.

Her statement depicted "Nobody will be spared". Prisca and the couple didn't feel the consequences of Susan's statement as much as Douglas and Molly did. Douglas melted into himself hopelessly as Molly halted every of her body's movements to comprehend what Susan said. Nonetheless, their fears and instincts beforehand never deceived them.

Prisca quietly took her car keys, pulled her shoes into her foot and left the house.

Immediately, Molly realized herself and blinked her eyes in a deranged manner. Prisca's attitude would have being considered wrong for she is expected to stay back to console Molly, plead with her friend to have mercy or sit down and mop. Unfortunately, the full understanding of courtesy differs to so many people.

This quickly reminded Molly of when Prisca reported her to Susan for joining the Tokex's band group. Prisca's daughter, Olivia was asked to leave the group by the coach because her performance wasn't good enough to be in the band. With that, she quickly ran to Susan and condemned every good thing the band group is reckoned with because Molly was retained.

Susan quickly warned and withdrew Molly from going for the band practices. From that time on, she labeled Prisca bad for ruining her participation in the only social group she joined successfully. Robin as well had his own bad records about Prisca which Susan always blatantly ignored for the sake of their friendship.

Molly is not surprised with her recent attitude because she never expected more from her.

"I'm sure she doesn't mean that?" Charles asked referring to Susan's decision as he pointed his right index finger to the stairs.

"She meant every bit of it," Douglas assured as Molly bursts into tears again, using her knee to support her elbow joints she covered her face with her palms, keeping her back in a slant position.

"I'm not surprised," he added as he placed his left hand on the arm of the sofa and supported his jaw with his fist.

Charles sighed as he leaned back on the sofa too. "So, what do we do?"

"I don't know," Molly replied as she tried to wipe her tears but still could not control its flow.

"Maybe we await her wrath," Douglas asserted giving up willingly

"No," Margie said sitting up, "I think you should talk to her Molly," she added as Molly looked up at her, "Yeah, I believe she will listen to you."

"She will not listen to her," Douglas assured.

"Please we should not conclude yet, until we give it a trial," Margie advised, "I believe she will listen." Douglas turned away his face in disagreement.

Few minutes later, Douglas left for his home while Charles and Margie headed home to get some rest.

Molly sincerely wished they will stay forever. Her burden was too many to carry alone. She thought of facing Susan's anger, fear from imaginations she already fabricated in her mind and nightmares of Robin's death.

As she turned and shut the door, a lonely sensation filled the sitting room. She purposely stood by the door for some time, backing it and holding its handle firmly. She used her eyes to survey every corner of the sitting room, rolling her bulgy eyeball from one property to another to make sure nothing will grip her from the back if she leaves the door handle. The door's handle became her fortress for some seconds.

Suddenly, she realized she wouldn't stand there forever. Then, she held her right index finger with her right thumb and index finger in fear as she gently walked back to her seat with no sound from the sole of her feet.

She carefully sat down; still looking back at the door she took as her defense in fear. She got confused of the sitting position to stay in order to defend herself quickly if need be. Engrossed by fear, she could see things that are unimaginable and hear sounds that never came from any source.

At this juncture, Molly's guilt ignited. She could hear Robin's and Susan's voice randomly, like though she is going crazy. She quickly held her ears with her hands and closed her eyes not to envisage such things; little did she know the mind on its own is a HD cinema that came play any sort of recorded memory or fear.

She quickly opened her eyes as she remembered vividly how Robin was breathing so hard to survive. The torments of fear she is passing through made her frown her face in discomfort and leaned back on the sofa she sat on hopelessly. She sluggishly stretched her legs vertically and shifted her head to the right as a way to give in to anything that wants to entrap her.

Her blames and regrets stood firmly before her. The lonely hands gripped her tight; she feels she is varnishing from her own self. Tears rolled down slowly from her left cornea, through her nose, down to her lips and jaw when she remembered she will not see Robin's face again. She sniffed and turned her head uprightly to resolve what next to do.

Molly's confusion came in different dimensions leaving her more biased and weakened.

She thought of going to bed to get some rest, but also knew Susan is not sleeping either, she thought of Margie's suggestion as she wiped her tears and bowed her head low a bit and thought of putting it into action."Mom will not listen," she said to herself. She looked up to the ceiling for answers on what to do but the ceiling remained mute too.

Then she began asking herself questions she could not answer. "Why did I accept Robin as my human subject in the first place?" "Why is mom silent about this? She didn't cry much, why didn't she wail and shout at us?" She wondered and brought her head down again to figure her questions out. As she questioned herself, it skipped her mind that silence could be a dangerous weapon too.

After few minutes of considering what to do, she decided to go and render an apology to Susan, to show how sorry she is and ascertain if she will pardon them. As she stood up slowly, her phone fell off from her lap; she reluctantly bent down and picked it, held it tightly as if to be her source of strength and hoped to be listened to.

As she walked up the stairs slowly to Susan's room, she felt her marrows melting away because her muscles lacked the ability and strength to carry her up to her destination. She kept rehearsing what she would say to her mother as she took each staircase.

When she got to her mother's room door, she stared at it still wishing all these hadn't happened. How did she get this far? Where would she go from here? She stood still at the door, her forehead against the door frame. No amount of words or tears would bring Robin back. And worst still, her mother would never forgive her of this crime, which she had to live with for the rest of her life.

After few minutes, she pulled away from the door frame,

took a deep breath and knocked.

"Come in," Susan said immediately making Molly to realize that she knew she was there all along. She opened the door gently, peeped around it to know where Susan is exactly. Then, she slowly limped in and carefully shot the door behind her.

"I'm listening," Susan said icily before Molly could say a word. The tone of her words brought tears again to Molly's eyes but she blinked them back. "I'm sure you wouldn't stand behind me to plead for mercy." Susan chided.

Molly stared at Susan who stood close to her bed, looking out of her window. It appeared she had been in that position since she came up. She looked grieved, but too quiet to let anyone understand what is in her mind or what she is passing through. She acts normal but in the real sense, dangerous. Molly sighed slowly, chanting a mantra in her head. "I have to do this."

Looking up at her mother, she said, "I'm sincerely sorry for all my research has cost you mom." Susan took a while to majestically respond to this.

"Clarify me on which you are pleading for: Robin's death? Or not telling me about the cloning trial?" She scolded folding her arms together underneath her breasts.

"Both," Molly replied shivering.

"Interesting," Susan paused and readjusted her arms interchangeably. "You know I always deceived myself about the peace you bring with you."

"Why are you so selfish Molly?" She asked expecting no reply as Molly bursts into tears. "You never imagined how I would feel even if this trial went well without my knowledge. All you cared for was to persuade your brother into this and drag him to his death."

"No, mom," Molly replied in tears as she knelt down immediately "I…"

"I do not need to listen to you Molly," she interrupted. "You have stepped on my fifth left toe Molly; it pains me so much because that's my most vulnerable toe."

"Robin was part of my hope in life Molly. Unfortunately, you took that hope away, I'm sorry I cannot let it be."

"I already contacted Vanessa, please go," she concluded and looked away as Molly looked up to her in surprise. She slowly stood up and left quietly.

As she closed the door behind her, she quickly held onto the wall on her right, leaned on it and swiftly slid down in a squatting position. She gradually pushed her hair backwards, holding her head to understand the depth of what she was into.

One will wonder who Vanessa is. Vanessa is one of the prominent and highly recommended legal practitioners in Gozax. Her educational success and achievements stands out amongst all. Shockingly, she has never lost any case since sworn into court. Her success in the law field makes people run after her no matter how much she charges. She is a powerful influence in the whole of Gozax.

Her non-sequential questioning in court can make an innocent client plead guilty unknowingly. Nothing passes her by, she leaves no stone unturned in her investigations. Her facial expressions always seem friendly with her lovely smiles, but she becomes venom when she wants to push one's head into the tight hole. Every verdict favors her client willingly. Unfortunately, Susan is hiring her.

Vanessa's success record piled up in Molly's mind as she stood up from the position she was in. She limped her way down the stairs, got tired and sat down on it. Tears refuse to fall out again, as she is hit by an intense headache. She considered herself doomed as she placed her hands on her head. Her fears and imaginations disappeared as all she thought about was how to prove her innocence.

Molly slowly stood up, supporting herself with the stair's reel, made her way to the sitting room and sat down.

"All I will do is to get some sleep," she advised herself hopelessly. She lay down on the sofa and slept off forgetting she was allocated to a room, she equally forgot Chokey at this moment of her troubles.

CHAPTER EIGHT

Neutral mother

Susan left the house very early before Molly woke up. A heavy knock on the door woke her up forcefully. She jumped up from the sofa almost falling and rushed to the door to open it with sleepy eyes. To her greatest surprise she beheld what she never expected in an early morning.

"Good morning, miss Molly," the Gozax's police officer who stood right in front of the door with his colleague greeted but got no reply as Molly kept turning around in confusion.

"I'm Officer Luke Dashaw," he said raising his identity card up to the level Molly could see it.

"You are under arrest for the murder of Robin Chopkins. Your hands please," he requested as she drew back.

"No, please there must be a mix up somewhere," she

pleaded. Officer Luke pulled out the handcuff clung to his belt holder and handcuffed her.

"Mom, mom, mom!" She called out three times looking up to the stairs for Susan to come out but she didn't. Then, they took her away.

The arrest came too sudden than she expected. "Mom, please help me," she thought as she sat in between two officers at the back seat of the police vehicle.

After they drove off, she became unperturbed by what was going on. Her silence, in that minute, depicted her as one that is not being charged of murder but she is really troubled inwardly. As she drew her right hand to her nose to wipe off some sweat spots, it occurred to her to put a call through to Douglas. She calmly turned to the officer by her right who seems to be approachable and said,

"Please I want to make a call?"

"Who do you want to call?"

"Mr. Douglas…"She replied quickly.

"He has been arrested too, no need to call him."

Molly looked stranded and trapped with the officer's reply. Her only solace available right now is Margie who could do little or nothing to save her. She felt so bad for involving Douglas in her cloning trial in the first place.

When the police vehicle took a turn to the right into Mamieu-Green Street, she caught sight of a young, blind, hunch-backed girl of adolescent age. She quickly turned back as the vehicle passed the helpless young girl who was playing her half shattered guitar happily with smiles on the pedestrian lane. Passersby kicked her unremorsefully as they went about their activities considering her insignificant.

As she lost sight of her, she gently turned. Molly tried as much as she could to puzzle out how life must be difficult for that young girl. No good food, water, clothes and shelter. No identifiable family, no support, good posture and eyesight.

"All my life, I have always lived in the shadows, blaming people for my weaknesses instead of accommodating and turning them into my strengths. This young girl has nothing to look up to but she is happily playing music not minding her miserable life condition." She thought. She looked out of the window.

"I didn't kill my beloved brother," she thought aloud.

This caught the attention of the officers that sat close to her and they turned almost at the same time to look at her

"You should save that for the court," the officer by her right mockingly said as the other laughed and turned away.

She looked up to the dashboard of the vehicle and saw a sticker that says, "Blame not yourself or anyone for life is complicated"

All of a sudden, strength from no source engulfed her. She drew her inspirations from the blind disabled young girl who still saw hope and beauty in life with her music despite her condition.

"I'm not blind, disabled or homeless neither am I living under palliative support, I'm so sorry and pained for Robin's death. I never planned things to turn out this way, neither did Robin, it is absolutely not my fault." She looked at the window, absorbed in her thoughts.

"After trial in court, if found guilty. Its either I'm hanged or life imprisoned, I didn't kill my brother."She bowed her head as the consequences went through her mind.

"I'm going to prison for now and not the grave yard, that's a bundle of hope for me. Robin, I remain ever grateful and indebted to you for this overwhelming sacrifice," she raised her head and closed her eyes.

"Words can't explain how much I value you my dear, but death came too sudden in a wrong way complicating things for me. Nonetheless, I promise to boldly inscribe your name on the sands of time. Rest on dear." She opened her eyes and it sparkled radiating so much strength, less guilt and confidence. A brand new Molly is unveiled.

As the driver pulled over at the right parking lot of Tokex D10 police station, the police officers quickly opened the back doors and stepped down as the officer by her right shot the door immediately while the other signaled her to come down.

As her left feet touched the ground, journalists and bloggers who are hunting for early morning events rushed to her. They asked her so many questions but the police officers blocked them and ordered her not to say a word to them. Initially, she was prepared to say nothing to anybody.

This moment, she assumes an extreme state of silence than Susan's because she took off her garments of guilt, fear and regrets to bear responsibility of her actions and decision with hope to be vindicated.

As the officers walked her to the station's entrance, the journalists bearing their microphones as well as the camera men still over crowded them slowing their pace.

Molly caught sight of Susan from afar and decided not to look towards her direction. Susan expected her to look gloomy and helpless but Molly turned out to be absolutely opposite of what she expected.

"Other police officers turned up and prevented the journalists from coming closer to the entrance as Molly walked elegantly into the station to Susan's surprise.

"She doesn't look grieved," Vanessa said with poise.

"Yeah," Susan replied in

surprise as she turned back to Vanessa.

"I see," Vanessa asserted raising her eyebrows. "I will file the case to the court and make other provisions." She assured as she held Susan's shoulder. "Take heart dear," she consoled and left.

Susan still turned back to be sure if it is the Molly that approached her hopelessly in tears at night that she was looking at.

"Babe, come and see this!" Charles shouted from the sitting room as he sipped from the cup of coffee in his left hand.

"Okay, I'm coming," Margie replied from the kitchen. Charles kept the cup of coffee on the center table, grabbed the remote and pressed 57 to change the channel. To his surprise, the same thing still appeared.

"It's everywhere," he said in a low tone as he placed his hands on his waist watching the television.

"Our correspondent who was at the police station this morning affirmed that miss Molly is presently in police custody awaiting trial," the newscaster reported as Charles scratched his beards with his right hand.

"What?" Margie interrupted. Charles turned to look at her. Margie quickly dropped her phone on the sofa and came closer to where Charles stood to confirm what she was seeing as the news headline.

"This is ridiculous," Charles lamented shaking his head.

"Susan seems not to have hesitated in charging her daughter to court for Robin's death. Still hang on as we…" the news caster stated.

"This is not just fair," Margie interrupted as she zipped her gown. "Susan can't be this heartless," Margie said before she rushed out of the sitting room angrily.

"Come on, where are you going to?" Charles asked following her immediately but not getting to her because of her fast moves.

"I'm going to give her a piece of my mind," she replied aggressively as she jammed the entrance door.

"Careful!" Charles advised as he stood still and gradually looked back to the television frowning.

To Margie it seemed unimaginable for a mother to sue her daughter to court although with justifiable reasons. She wondered why Susan keeps persuading her to have children with Charles while she adamantly frustrates her daughter with the unthinkable.

"Molly cannot hurt a fly," she spoke out dourly as she opened the gate wide enough to enable Charles's car pass through.

She quickly rushed back to the car with few steps almost running. She entered the car,

and dropped her purse on the first passenger's seat. Just then, she realized she didn't collect the car key.

She sighed in frustration and rushed back into the house.

"Babe is that you? How did it go?" Charles inquired from the bathroom as he scrubbed his neck not minding she came back early.

"Yeah, I came back for the car key," she replied and rushed out again.

As she drove, by passing the traffic jams. She still pondered on how to interrogate Susan's action. All she wants to prove is Molly's vulnerability to depression in the whole scenario even if she does not prove her innocence beyond all doubts.

At the same time, she wishes she is a lawyer so that she could stand up proudly against Susan and prove her wrong through every means she could.

"Be careful not to be arrested this morning Margie," she advised herself as she recklessly over took a diesel tanker, almost hitting a bus crossing her lane to the other lane directly opposite Ma Lache eatery.

Susan went home to prepare for work, not long after Molly got to the police station. Coincidentally, she drove into her compound at the same time as Prisca.

"Hey," Prisca greeted as she got down from her car holding her hand bag on her left hand.

"Hey," Susan replied forcing herself to look OK as she closed her car's door.

"How are you this morning?"

"I'm better," Susan answered as they walked up the stairs to the entrance door together.

"I heard Molly has been arrested." Prisca questioned as she opened the door for Susan to enter first.

"Thank you," she appreciated her kind gesture as she entered the house. "The police came for her this morning."

"Cool," Prisca asserted as she dropped her bag on the sofa. She then progressed to the kitchen to make coffee.

Susan gently numbered her footstep to the dinning. "What is so cool about my daughter's arrest?" she wondered as she placed her right hand on the dining table.

She quickly kicked Prisca's utterance off her mind when she considered words can possess different meanings sequel to the context they are used in. She slowly pulled her hair backwards as Margie barged into the house unannounced. Margie's entrance made her turn quickly to see who it is. At the sight of Margie, she wondered why she came in such a manner.

"Good morning," Margie greeted with a malicious face as she walked to her.

"Good morning, how are you Margie?" Susan replied trying to ignore her abnormal attitude and terrifying entrance.

"I am fine," she answered as she shuffled her car key through both hands.

"And Cha…"

"Charles is fine," she interrupted.

"Okay," Susan said as she turned to the wall directly opposite her. She already figured out what Margie's attitude is all about.

"I saw the news headline this morning," Margie said as she drew closer to Susan.

"What about it?"

"Everything about it is wrong, Susan," Margie answered almost raising her voice as Prisca came to the dining unnoticed. "Molly does not deserve what she is getting from you."

"She killed my son, Margie," Susan replied with anger.

"You mean with a gun?" She asked but got no answer. "Your allegation against her is baseless, you are wrong, Susan," she added furiously in a loud tone. Susan smiled and turned away again

"Molly can be awkward at times but can't hurt the tiniest being inexistence not to talk of her brother."

"Robin died out of medical complication that arose during the cloning trial which was unfortunately beyond the medical team to handle, not Molly's fault," She added raging with anger again.

"Margie, for the fact that Molly kept everything about the trial away from me makes it her fault," Susan shouted at her

"Did you ask why?" Margie shouted back.

"Obviously not, because she knows I wouldn't have permitted it and Robin's death automatically makes her reasons irrelevant," Susan replied quickly in a high tone.

"Interesting," Margie said tonelessly. She slowly held up her car key in her palms, staring at it steadily, she said, "This very action makes you putridly horrible and heartless Susan."

"I wonder how you expect me to take your advice to have children with Charles when you can't cherish the lovely bird you have at hand." She stared back at Susan as Susan stared at her too.

"The least thing Molly expected from this cloning trial was Robin's death. That trial was like a medium to substantiate her existence. I really wish you could believe that." She paused for a while.

"Having her jailed and to face trial does not bring you an inch to be counted as a mother," she lamented as Susan bowed her head listening calmly to her."I came…" she continued.

"Justifying Robin's death makes her more of a mother Margie," Prisca interrupted her. "Molly is totally wrong and deserves every bit of what she is getting right now," she concluded. Susan turned her attention to her, why was Prisca so happy about Molly's arrest? She wondered still staring at Prisca strangely.

Prisca chipping into Margie's discussion with Susan would be one of the biggest regrets of her life. Margie rejoiced for the prey has fallen into the predator's trap

"Tell me more dear," Margie requested smiling as she slowly turned to Prisca ready to pick up any arrow of revolt she vomits and strike it against her.

"Molly should have considered the detrimental consequences of involving Robin in that trial without Susan's consent before she embarked on it, that makes her less of a daughter dear," Prisca replied proudly as she sipped from the cup of coffee she bore in her left hand feeling.

Surprisingly, Margie lacked words to use against her because to dialogue with her wasn't her prior aim of coming to Susan's house

"You see; I have nothing to say to you Prisca because I can absolutely identify a wolf in the flock when I see one," Margie replied starkly as she drew closer to her.

"Not forgetting," she continued moving her right index finger sideways.

"You are the most pathetic, selfish, heartless whore I have ever encountered in my life," Margie concluded insolently and turned to Susan.

"Watch your words young woman," Prisca warned cruelly.

"Or what?" She said, then to Susan, "Who is she?" When she got no reply, she continued, "I guess your dear friend."

She cast a glance at Prisca and returned her attention to Susan, "Quote me anywhere tomorrow; she will squeeze your head into your doom soonest, Susan." With that she picked up her bag and left. Prisca was staring daggers at her.

Margie's last statement clearly left Susan with too many questionable thoughts about Prisca.

For some seconds after Margie left, Susan ruminated over her advice and statements. She recalled several times she has gotten warnings about Prisca but ignored it. Susan seems to be blind to the awful sides of Prisca that others see. Literally, she acts like she is under her spell such that she tolerates all her suspicious attitudes in the name of friendship.

Molly and late Robin never respected their friendship due to Prisca's alarming jealousy about them. Unfortunately, Susan is extremely insensitive to that. As usual, she paid deaf ears to Margie's warning and took it as an outcome of misconceived perceptions towards Prisca. When she looked up, she noticed Prisca busy with her phone.

"The coffee please," Susan requested.

"Oh," Prisca acclaimed and handed over the coffee to her.

"Nice bangle," Susan complimented looking at her wrist.

"Thanks" she replied with a forced smile as she shifted the phone over to her left hand and raised her right wrist to throw a glance at the bangle. "Uhmm, I will have to run along because of work," she added as she quickly turned to leave. "Hope you called Eric to inform him of this?"

"Yes, I already called him and some other staff that I won't be coming for work. Eric personally asked me to stay for three days," Susan replied and

noticed the change in Prisca's mood.

"Cool," Prisca replied almost soundlessly.

"Hey," Susan called calmly as she stood up hastily and followed her.

"I apologize for Margie's attitudes, please forgive her. Her utterances are simply youthful excesses we have to overlook." Prisca collected her handbag on the sofa.

"It's ok, I understand," Prisca accepted still trying to smile as Susan nodded in agreement. "I will have to go now," she added as she took few steps close to Susan and held her left elbow.

"Do take good care of yourself dear," she concluded as Susan opened her arms wide enough and hugged her.

"I will," Susan said as they still held each other's shoulder.

Margie got home and realized the house was lonely and got worried.

"Baby?"She called out as she came out of the bedroom wondering where he is. After a while of searching, Margie opened her purse which she kept on the dining table and dialed his number.

"Hey, where are you?" She asked curiously as soon as she heard Charles's voice.

"I'm at work," he replied.

"Oh," she said as she rested on the dining table. "I'm sorry I kept you waiting."

"Don't be dear, how did it go?"

"Nothing much," Margie replied, "I told her the truth she needs to know about her actions and she seems undisturbed. While, Prisca got her own share too," She explained "I think I can explain better when we are together."

"Ok, are you still feeling feverish?" He inquired because Margie complained of having fever early in the morning.

"No, I'm feeling better now. I have to go and see Molly to know how she is doing and also find out her plan," she concluded

"Ok, that's cool, we will talk later then. Take care."

"Yeah, you too, I love you," she said and hung up the call.

Few minutes after Charles settled into the office, Tom came in.

"Hey, man," Tom greeted.

"Hey, good morning," Charles replied as he quickly dropped his phone on his table to welcome Tom's handshake. "How is Dorcas and Shirley this morning?"

"My little angel is cute and my beautiful wife is fine and cute too," Tom replied as they laughed out loud.

Tom never ceases to chant Dorcas's good qualities wherever he goes. Actually, Tom and Charles had formed the *Lucky Hubby Gang* at Buzz soft vicinity. Tom and

Charles's litany of praise for their wives can make one get jealous and indulge in comparing his spouse to theirs.

Amazingly, they not only share their peaceful moments with their wives but also tables the awful and dramatic times as well. Nevertheless, they will always admit to how lucky they are to have their wives.

Tom and Charles became good friends ever since Charles started working at Buzz soft and admitted he is a lucky man pertaining to his marital partner. Their friendship got tighter over the years and rapidly extended to their wives. Most married men in the institution will always leave them angrily whenever they start their Lucky Men anthem.

To Tom and Charles, it meant nothing but a way to appreciate how privileged they are to be with their wives.

"And Mag?" Tom quickly asked as he pulled up his trouser although fastened with belt.

"She is fine," Charles replied as stretched out his left hand and pulled out a file from his shelf.

"How is her friend coping with the arrest?"

"Who told you that?" Charles quickly asked as he turned to hand over the file to Tom.

"Don't give me that look, the news is everywhere. At least I have a television," Tom queried as he stood erect and redressed his collar.

"Fine, she is in police custody. Poor Molly," Charles replied.

"Susan went too far," Tom lamented.

"It baffles me how some people can be so hard heartened," Charles said. "Initially, Molly and Robin are wrong for keeping the cloning trial away from Susan, but Susan should have treated this as a family issue, listened to Molly's reasons and know the way forward." Tom nodded in affirmation.

"You know I was at their residence with Margie on the night of the incidence," he continued.

"Really?"

"Yeah, she promised them that she will deal with them with everything in her," Charles mentioned as Tom listened keenly.

"Wow, that sounds severe," Tom replied with surprise as Charles continued immediately.

"At first, I thought she didn't mean it although Molly and Douglas confirmed it, I still doubted them until this morning's news headline emerged," he narrated.

"She also went ahead to hire VV," Tom added smiling playfully.

"VV? What's that?" Charles asked interestedly.

CHAPTER NINE

The unexpected little friend

"Venomic Vanessa," Tom shouted with his eyes wide open to express the energy that accompanies the name as they laughed.

"Yeah, that's another challenge to tackle," Charles stated as he caressed his forehead.

"No, it is not," Tom said as he stood up to move to his table.

"What is it then?"

"That's deep shit," Tom asserted and they laughed again.

"Please have this file Billy dropped for you to work on," Charles handed it over to him.

"I heard the Rosary Man was also arrested?" Tom inquired as he collected the file and picked up his brief case from Charles's table.

"Rosary Man? Who's that?"

"Are you sure you reside in this town?"

"Yes of course," Charles laughed.

"No, I don't think so," Tom doubted as he dropped his brief case on his shelf and sat down.

"Stop it," Charles said and paused to think. "Oh, you mean Douglas?" He asked smiling.

"Yes," Tom answered as they laughed again. "That's what baby Shirley calls him," he added amidst laughter.

"Why?" Charles investigated amidst laughter too.

"I don't know, maybe because of his titanic Rosary," he answered as they laughed.

"He is quite close with the kids in Mamieu-Gold, so they named him that for his obvious Rosary and he gathers them to pray the Rosary with him during evening hours, Shirley goes too."

"Really, that's nice. Douglas is indeed an honest man; I respect him so much," Charles adorned as he dragged his seat closer to the table to face the day's work.

"Yeah, he is…" Tom confirmed as Carly interrupted immediately distracting them from what they are doing. The standing position she assumed at the door made Tom to question her immediately

"Why are you standing like that over there, this is an office please," he questioned as Carly laughed and walked into the office majestically.

"Relax, don't be so mean. Moreover, I can't take Dorcas's place," she said and smiled naughtily.

"I'm sure you can't," Tom replied as he casts back his gaze on the file he is working on.

"Good morning Charles," she greeted looking at him intently.

"Good morning Carly," he

replied sparing no time for further conversations.

"Hey, Billy," She greeted as Billy walked into the office.

"Hey, baby, how are you doing?" He replied as they hugged each other.

"I'm fine dear," she responded as they let go of each other.

"How was your night?" Billy asked again with a bold smile.

"Awesome," she replied softly.

"I can see that. You look Gorgeous," Billy admired.

"Thank you," she replied feeling flattered. "You don't look bad either."

"Really, Thanks," Billy appreciated gallantly.

"I have to go dear. Take care," she added and left as Billy still looked back to watch her walk away. Tom and Charles noticed his lustful gaze at her but still minded their businesses.

"Good morning Charles," Billy greeted immediately he lost sight of Carly.

"Good morning, how are you doing?"

"I'm good," Billy replied and walked to Tom's desk.

"Hey, did you get the file?" He asked Tom as he stretched out his hands to shake him too but was stopped.

"Calm down, why did you stop smiling when you turned to us?" Tom queried looking keenly at Billy to see his reaction.

"We are not Carly," Charles answered on his behalf smiling.

"Oh that. Of course, I can't smile at you," Billy said with a smile showing his right palm.

"Why?" Tom asked curiously as he closed the file, holding onto the page he is working on.

"Because I am not gay," he replied confidently

"Yeah, you are not gay but still remember you are married," Charles advised cautiously.

"Exactly," Tom affirmed in agreement with Charles as he opened the file again to continue with his work.

"Oh please," he replied reluctantly to Charles's advice as he caught sight of his file in Tom's hands. "Good thing you have the file," he added immediately to put an end to their former topic of discussion. "Hope everything in there is clear to you?"

"Yes," Tom replied and continued going through the file not distracted by Billy's presence and questions.

"Good," he said as he clapped his hands once gladly. "Any questions?"

"How is your wife?" Tom asked sluggishly still focused on the file.

"Skip, next question," he said frowning.

"How is your wife?" Tom asked again stressing his words slowly as he mentioned them one after the other to Billy's hearing.

"Fuck you," he replied and left angrily as Tom and Charles burst into laughter.

Margie had slept on the sofa for almost an hour. She woke up when she heard the doorbell ring. Then, she sluggishly sat up and walked weakly to the door to open it.

"Good morning, please how did you get in here?" She asked looking around.

"Good morning, the gate is open," the delivery man replied.

"Oh," she uttered as she made her way to lock it.

"I have locked it ma," he answered smiling. She turned to look at him in surprise.

"Really, thanks," she said wondering what he was up to.

Her facial expression suddenly changed as she touched the front and back pockets of her trouser and unfortunately could not feel her phone. She began feeling trapped as she is not with her phone with which she could reach out for help.

Additionally, the strange man locked the gate by himself. Margie smartly fixed a confident eye contact with him and summoned courage to question him.

"How may I help you?" She asked curiously as the man suddenly realized himself and presented the file he came with to her.

"Uhmm, I am from Sun Print insurance company. I came for your husband to fill and sign his health insurance document," he said as he opened the file for Margie to glance through it.

Margie takes her time to move close to him noticeably.

Firstly, she thought of when Charles ventured into health insurance without her consent. Secondly, why would the signature be appended at home and not called up to their office? Thirdly, all signing and enquiries should have been made on the first day he went to their company. Also, he didn't dress formerly. Lastly, he didn't show his identification card.

All these piled up in her mind in few seconds as she kept drawing closer to him.

She suddenly became conscious of his hands, pen and everything he has to ensure her defense mechanism before he makes a move.

As she kept drawing closer, almost a glance at the document; it suddenly occurred to her to ask for his identification card.

"Your ID please," she requested.

"Oh, please pardon my misconduct," he apologized smiling as he puts his right hand into his breast pocket and showed his ID to her.

"Okay," she said in confirmation.

She relaxed a bit and took the document from him and started going through it. Suddenly, she spoke up.

"I'm sorry this is the wrong residence," she noticed as she points at the residence number. "This is residence 39 but the document is for residence 38."

"Oh, I'm so sorry madam," he apologized as he collected the document.

"It's ok," Margie accepted. "That is residence 38," she pointed at the next compound by the right.

"Okay. Thank you."

"You are welcome, let me see you to the gate," Margie added with relief.

"Okay," he said as they walked to the gate.

Margie still didn't lose guard of herself knowing quite well that anything could happen. As they walked, he quickly turned to Margie's shock.

"What?" She quickly asked curiously.

"You look gorgeous and principled ma," he smiled.

"Thank you," she said smiling back forcefully.

"Yeah," he uttered and continued moving.

When he stepped out of the gate, she ignored his goodbye wave, shot the gate and leaned on it placing her right hand on her chest in relief. Then, she remembered she scheduled to see Molly when she gets home.

"Oh, my God," Margie shouted and ran back into the house. She hurriedly picked up her phone on the sofa she laid on. Immediately, she caught sight of the wall clock and it said 10:53am.

"Wow," she acclaimed as she grabbed her purse and car key and rushed out again.

When Molly entered the cell, she carefully took her time to look at everything in the cell. The ash-colored wall, the white-wooden bench by her left, the white bulb that illuminated the cell located in the middle of the ceiling right above her head from where she stood. Every other thing seemed plain, and then she noticed the locked jail protector behind her.

She turned slowly and carefully observed the edges and rods of the jail protector. Then, she moved closer to it and held two rods with her hands, one on each hand and pushed her face out a bit through the space in between the rods.

Molly held onto the rods firmly and bowed her head, she felt bad for being where she never expected to be in her life. She felt dejected as she closed her eyes and tightened her fist on the rods. As she wallowed in her grief, a strange little soft voice beckoned on her. "Hey!"

She opened her eyes immediately and saw a little girl jailed in the cell directly opposite hers.

"Hey!" She responded with surprise.

"I guess this is your first time in jail?" The little girl inquired.

"Yeah, maybe," Molly replied in pretense.

"It is obvious," the girl said and looked away.

"Why are you here?" Molly interestedly asked as she knelt down in her cell to the girl's size.

"I stabbed my mom with a kitchen knife," she replied bluntly.

"What? Wow, that's bad," Molly concluded truthfully raising her eyebrows.

"Yeah, it is bad," she said as she speedily stood up to face Molly with anger. Molly seemed confused because she never expected such bitterness and fury to emanate from a child of that age.

"I did it because I have endured her ruthless attitude towards my daddy for years now," she added as her anger and voice tone increased.

"She takes advantage of my daddy because she is older, makes him cook and do the house chores, while she sleeps lazily, cheats on him, fights him confidently because she is bigger, talks to him arrogantly, orders him around and treats him like a baby.

All she does is to go out late in the evening and come back early in the morning to bark like a dog," she raged non-stop as Molly signaled her to reduce her voice.

The girl ignored her. "She sleeps all day and goes out for her disgusting business in the evening. Young lady if you are in my shoes you will do the same."

"Please calm down," Molly pleaded. "I'm sorry for…"

"What's going on there?" One of the officers shouted from the station's counter

"Nothing, we are good," Molly replied and stayed calm for another question but got none.

After a while, she continued her conversation with the little girl.

"I'm sorry; you have to go through all that. What's your name?" Molly asked passionately.

"Olivia," the girl replied reluctantly.

"Beautiful name, how old are you?" Molly asked again as she sat down at the right edge of cell to communicate well with her.

"Why do you ask like you care?" She questioned aggressively.

"How old are you, Olivia?" Molly repeated her question staring at her.

"How is that relevant?" She questioned again meanly.

"Because I want to know,"

"I am eight years old," she answered in a low tone looking towards another direction.

"Cool," Molly said, "coincidentally, we are the same."

"Really?" Olivia replied with her eyes wide open as she knelt down in front of her jail protector holding two rods with her hands. "You hate your mom too?"

"No," Molly replied.

"Then why are you her?"

"She believes I killed my brother through a cloning trail," Molly replied.

"Did you?"

"No," Molly answered innocently as Olivia quietly sits down.

"What is cloning by the way?" She asked ignorantly.

"Cloning is the process of copying or collecting special genetic qualities of a particular organism to sophisticate another organism and make them have and exhibit the copied qualities of the original organism." Molly explained plainly for her to understand.

"Wow, so you copied animals' genes into your brother or what?"

"Yes," Molly affirmed smiling.

"Did he behave like an animal?" She asked innocently with her eyes wide open glittering with doubts to be cleared.

"Yes," Molly answered smiling boldly..

"Wow, that's amazing," she stated in astonishment."But why your brother?" She added frowning.

"I needed a human subject for a cloning trial, he submitted himself to be one, to honor my dad and make my research a success. Unfortunately, he died in the process of the trial due to an uncontrolled medical complication," Molly narrated sadly and bowed her head.

"I'm so sorry," Olivia sympathized. "But why is your mom so angry to jail you. Basically, it's not your fault," she added as Molly looked at her and smiled.

"You are so smart," Olivia smiled gently, "Because we didn't tell her about the cloning trial," Molly replied faintly.

"Why?" She asked curiously.

"My dad died horribly during cloning too, she wouldn't have permitted it if we told her," Molly explained in a low tone as she looked at her.

"Wow, so you hate your mom right now?" Olivia inquired concentrating her gaze on Molly.

CHAPTER TEN

Team MOM

"No," Molly replied smiling as she adjusted her position to suit her comfort.

"Why?" She asked surprisingly as the question and answer section continued.

"Because I had a beautiful encounter this morning," Molly replied and paused for a while. "As we were driving to this place in the police vehicle, I saw a badly disabled blind girl smiling and playing music with her untidy guitar on the pedestrian lane along Mamieu-Green. I drew my inspiration from her. Despite her life challenges, she still played music with so much hope neglecting all her difficulties."

"I decided to blame nobody for any situation I find myself in rather accommodate my pains and create my joy and happiness in it. No matter how bad it is." Molly added looking back at Olivia.

"Wow, I will love to see her someday," Olivia replied feeling encouraged.

"You will, I will show you to her," Molly assured as Olivia became gloomy.

"Only if I will leave here, I miss my dad," she lamented bitterly.

"Don't feel that way, you will definitely get out of here in due time," Molly consoled her convincingly.

"Why are you here instead of the juvenile rehabilitation institute?" Molly asked curiously.

"They said I need a lawyer," she replied frowning.

"Ok, does your dad come to see you regularly?"

"No, he is not allowed. Just Beatrice my dad's aunt."

"Okay, cheer up. This isn't your fault. All will be well soon," Molly assured smiling.

"Ok, thank you," she replied feeling better. "Please be my friend?" Olivia asked childishly.

"Sure, I'm your friend," Molly replied as they smiled at each other.

"Your name?" She asked happily with bold smiles.

"Oh, forgive me. I am Molly."

"Nice." Olivia smiled.

Their friendship began flourishing rapidly. Although, they are separated from each other but it isn't a barrier to them. They connected with each other as if they knew themselves long before meeting again in jail.

Olivia told her everything she knows about herself, school, and family. She could also tell her the size and length of her intestines if it was possible. Molly flowed with her level of understanding and mode of discussion with ease. She feels relaxed even though it was in jail; the loneliness that gripped her on her initial entrance into the cell had disappeared.

Most of their discussions were based on question and answers setting to enable Olivia understand most things Molly said. As their discussion got intense so did happiness and freedom they are presently entitled to filled the air.

In as much as they reduced their vocal volume not to attract the attention of the police officers on duty. They still laugh out involuntarily and quickly cover their mouths in panic.

For the moments their cheerful discussion lasted, they forgot their captivity, all that mattered was just the sweet stories they told each other. Molly shared ugly experiences she had while growing up, not neglecting the intervention of her savior in all of them.

"Pox pushed my head into the ice-cream I was having for lunch," Molly shared sadly, smiling at the same time.

"Wow, that's unfair," she commented.

"Yeah, he was indeed a pox," Molly confirmed.

"If I were you I would have beaten the hell out of the God forsaken bully," Olivia challenged proudly.

"It's not that easy girl, he is tall, fat which made him look older and bigger than his age. Even though we were in the same class, I still feared his deep voiced orders. All thanks to Margie who surfaced from nowhere and beat him up mercilessly," Molly defended herself.

"Yeah, Margie surely deserves an award," she said still not smiling.

"More than an award, I believe she will soon be here," Molly concluded happily.

"That's only if they will allow her," Olivia stated and paused for a while, moping at Molly sheepishly.

"What?" Molly asked.

"I'm imagining your face with patches of ice-cream. So weird," She bursts into laughter.

"Stop, you are beginning to be insolent," Molly warned jokingly.

"I'm sorry I can't help it," Olivia said amidst laughter and suddenly stops to say something. "In my school, I do not bully and I don't tolerate bullies too."

"Really, that's great," Molly congratulated.

"Yeah, kudos to my friends, Didi and Mark. They coached me in all street fighting techniques," she added confidently.

"Didi and Mark deserve to be awarded too," Molly chipped in as she bursts into laughter, feeling she has gotten back to Olivia.

"Yeah," Olivia replied frowning and feeling degraded.

"I have other friends too," Molly spoke up as she noticed Olivia become icy.

"What kind of friends? Guardian angels?" She asked mockingly and laughed.

"No, animal friends," Molly replied.

"Animal friends? How?" Olivia asked amidst confusion. "Do you speak with animals? Do you understand them?"

She innocently forwarded her questions because from her experience so far, she has seen humans communicate with animals only in cartoons. For Molly to have mentioned she has animal friends definitely means she is extraordinary. She quickly knelt down to look Molly in the eyes and discover her answer. Her inquisitiveness stiffed her posture and gaze as she awaited Molly's response.

"Relax, they are just animal statues," Molly replied smiling.

Olivia hissed heavily and sat

down forcefully in disappointment.

"What? Molly asked in surprise of the strange attitude. "They keep me company, I talk to them when I'm depressed, though they don't talk back but I feel…"

"Whatever you feel is abnormal," Olivia shouted as she interrupted Molly to her surprise. "How do you talk to animals?" She asked strangely expecting no answer. "I understand you are obsessed with animals but talking to them is totally ridiculous and unimaginable."

Molly stared at her. "What?" Olivia questioned meanly.

"Come on, it is my life and has absolutely nothing to do with whatever you think. To increase your pain, I also named them; Chokey, Giant tiger and Cat," Molly bragged as Olivia covered her ears with her hands to show loss of interest.

They continued chatting and laughing until Margie walked in unexpectedly.

"Hey," Margie greeted with wet eyes at the sight of Molly in the cell.

"Hey," Molly replied smiling as she quickly stood up from the floor on which she sat chatting with Olivia.

For a while, they stood moping at each other. Margie just couldn't believe her eyes. The least place she expected her dear friend to be was in a jail. They always discussed about places they will go and places they wouldn't step their foot on. Molly's most dreaded place was jail. Margie searched for words to say to her but lost all. Unfortunately, this time she is partially unable to save her.

All this while, Molly and Olivia chatted freely. All her troubles phased away but immediately Margie stepped in, she had that cold bath of troubles again.

Although, filled with joy to see Margie; her old self resurfaced again. It dawned on her once more that she is imprisoned.

They suddenly got dumb, unable to locate the right words to say to each other. Margie's purse kept dangling although attached to a narrow handle which Molly held with her index finger. Her helplessness stood her still at the same position moping at Molly.

Olivia could understand their states of emotions and sat quietly by the right edge of her cell's wall monitoring them closely

Suddenly, Molly realized herself and remembered the new Molly does not want to be pitied for any reason.

"Hey, come here," Molly suddenly spoke up as she puts her hands through the jail protector to hug her. Margie speedily rushed into her arms, putting her hands through as well to hug her.

Immediately, the patiently waiting tears that had gathered round her eyes matched down her cheeks gloriously. Molly couldn't hold back her tears as she heard Margie sniffing. It pained her so much because this is the first time they hugged each other in tears of troubles and separated yet close to each other.

Margie cried harder because of her inability to help. The first time she feels handicapped on Molly's case. As they poured down their tears on each other's shoulder, they totally forgot Margie is being timed.

"You both should let go of the tears and think of better chances of getting her out of here," Olivia chipped in wisely interrupting the emotional display.

"Margie, it's okay," Molly said as she opened her reddened eyes on hearing Olivia's advice. She tried as much as she can to release herself from Margie but she still held her tightly.

"I'm sorry, Molly," she apologized blaming herself. "This is not your fault," Molly said as Margie finally let go of her.

"I'm ashamed of myself. I…" Margie said with a shaking voice still blaming herself.

"Hey, it's ok," Molly quickly interrupted as she wiped her tears with her hands.

"You shouldn't be blaming yourself right now, rather be my strength and struggle to get me out of here in one piece," Molly spurred her holding her shoulder.

"I'm sorry I can't stand this. I just can't help it," Margie stated as she cried the more.

"Hey stop, come here," Molly said as she drew her closer and began wiping her tears by herself.

"Listen, I might look doomed right now but there are still chances for me to get out of here victoriously, please be actively and strongly part of this scheme Margie, be my life saver."

"We will surely conquer this," Molly added looking at her intently.

"Yeah," Margie supported as she wiped her tears. "That's my best friend."

"We will prove my innocence together, ok?" Molly asked expecting Margie's full pledge of alliance.

"Yeah sure, the Ms?"She replied raising her index finger to signal the slogan they use when challenged. "Will always surf through," Molly completed as they made the tip of their index fingers touch one another as they hugged each other tightly again.

They loosed hold of each other's warmth feeling energized and motivated to fight for Molly's vindication tirelessly. They kept smiling at each other for some seconds as they held their hands together, sealing their solidarity for each other.

The fact that they suddenly inculcated in themselves the power inherent in standing up for each other's justice and rights despite their weaknesses made them wax their confidence strongly.

"I promise to get you out of here," Margie pledged.

"I know," Molly declared smiling.

"So what's up? What's with this new Molly?" They had totally forgotten Olivia's presence, yet she didn't bother to intrude.

"Oh! My bad, Please meet Olivia, my little friend," Molly introduced her.

Just then Margie realized there is a beautiful creature behind her and quickly knelt down in front of Olivia.

"Wow, what are you doing here?" Margie asked curiously as she caressed her right cheek.

"It's kind of complicated," Molly chipped in trying to save Olivia the explanation.

"Yeah, consequences of a terrible home," Olivia added reluctantly

"I'm so sorry dear," Margie said. "You will be fine," she assured.

"Yeah, I know. You are indeed a life saver, kind hearted and always sorry," Olivia complimented as they all laughed.

"I guess Molly has told you a lot."

"Yes, a whole lot," Olivia replied.

"She has been my solitude and gossip mate," Molly said.

"I see, that's interesting; at least making the situation less tight and horrible," Margie asserted as she stood up from where she knelt, backing the main entrance to the cells in order to communicate with them easily.

"Yeah," Molly affirmed smiling back.

"You know; I think we should form a team," Olivia suggested childishly.

"Really?" Margie said surprised.

"Yeah, team MOM," she added convincingly as the other two stared at each other.

"Hmmm, team MOM?" Molly and Margie chorused astonishingly.

"Yeah, like team Margie, Olivia and Molly. That makes sense right?"She asked joyfully as she smiled boldly at both of them.

"Yeah," Molly supported.

Although, it sounded awkward, they quickly accepted as she presently believes strongly in team efforts no matter how insignificant it maybe.

"Yeah, team MOM," Margie also accepted as they laughed happily.

CHAPTER ELEVEN

Be calm, I'm here

Their discussion got deeper and deeper into things they will never mention to a young girl like Olivia. Suddenly, Molly remembered someone very important to her, then she hurriedly turned to Margie and asked interestedly.

"How is Douglas? Have you heard from him? One of the police officers told me he was arrested before me?"

"Yeah, he was arrested in the church premises while he stepped out of the church after morning mass," Margie narrated scratching her forehead as Molly slowly sat down on the floor and drew backwards to rest her back on the wall behind her

"Come on, don't feel that way, Molly," Margie calmly said as she swiftly sat down on the corridor to console her.

"His arrest must be a shameful one," Molly lamented piteously. "I saw him first before coming here, he is fine dear," Margie assured holding Molly's shoulder.

"Really?" Molly enquired immediately lifting her back from the wall on which she rested.

"Yes, he is totally fine. He asked of you and instructed me to make sure you are Ok," she stated as Molly rested back on the wall again.

"I wish I didn't involve him in all this," Molly lamented as she bowed her head.

"It's ok Molly, Douglas is fine, and you worry too much."

"I wish Robin didn't die in the first place. Everything would have been normal. No infliction of mom's wrath, no arrest, no jail, no court appearances and possibly no imprisonment," Molly worried frowning.

"Stop please," Margie pleaded as she drew closer to her looking low-spirited.

"Robin I miss you so much," she said and paused as Margie kept consoling her. "I still remember all his favorite songs and raps."

"Really?" Marge asked. "Come on, it's still very early to forget," Molly emphasized.

"Yeah, that's right," Margie retorted as she tilted her neck down.

"You remember one of his favorite rap songs *God has gat my back* by Joe Lax?" Molly asked still smiling.

"Yes I do," Margie admitted as Molly started singing it as soon as she got her response, then Margie joined.

"I'm gonna win in all I can,

because God has gat my back,

the shameless fishes try na ditch me,

but ain't gonna give in,

so they know I'm not a weakling,

God's gat my back (2X)

Yeah my foot prints a powerfully covered" they both sang joyfully amidst so much pain in memory of Robin

"Another one by Silas Kiosk. *Be calm, I'm here,*" Molly hastily reminded as they sang again to Olivia's delight

"*Amidst all troubles dear one,*

keep calm and know I'm here

if the troubles rage gets tougher

quickly whisper to the nearest cool breeze

I miss you dear

be calm my dear for just in a jiffy

ripples of my love for you

will come directly to your heart

to adorn you with peace

absolute peace, so be calm my dear for I'm here

So be calm my dear for I'm here (2X)" They sang amidst tears.

"That's deep" Olivia commented sadly

"I miss you Robin," Molly whispered to thin air, believing its going somewhere, and then she closed her eyes and tears rushed down her cheeks

"Rest on Robin," Margie said as she wiped her tears with her sleeves.

Just then one of the police officers on duty came in and notified Margie that her duration is over.

"Oh," Margie asserted in surprise of how fast the time could be. "Just a minute please," she said as she knelt down immediately in front of Molly.

"I will make arrangements for your lawyer, everything will be fine trust me," she assured maintaining a direct eye contact with Molly.

"Okay," Molly replied as she nodded in affirmation

"Do not worry about Douglas, he already has a lawyer," she added as she held Molly's hands. "I will miss you dear, you have Olivia to hang on with. Be strong, I will be back soon," Margie said as she stood up to leave, while the police officer waited.

"Take care dear," Molly said as they hugged each other tightly.

"I will, you too," Margie said as they unglued from each other.

Then she turned to Olivia smiling with patches of hope all over her face. "Hey, your face is bravely inscribed in my heart. Take good care of yourself. All will be fine soon, I mean very soon. I'm sure you are in good hands."

"Thanks," Olivia appreciated as they hugged each other.

"Madam, please leave," the officer warned meanly.

"Alright, I have to go. Team MOM," Margie said smiling. "Team MOM!" Olivia and Molly chorused as they bid goodbye and the police officer escorted her out of the cell section.

Margie walked out of the police station with so much relief and optimism to start something in fight for Molly's justice. While walking to her car, she thought of so many lawyers she knew who could put up strong defense strategies for Molly."

Unfortunately, all of her options got disqualified either because of bad legal practice reputation or high service charge. She sluggishly stepped close to the driver's door and stopped when attorney Patrick Bee popped into her mind

"Hmmm," she muttered to herself as she rested her arms directly on top of the car's roof. Patrick over the years has gathered good legal defense records for himself. His efforts in standing for the truth and advocating for the less privileged has earned him so much honor and respect from the populace.

His resilient fight for the voiceless summed up to the accolades of respect he gets from the whole of Gozax.

Accordingly, Margie doubted if he will accept to stand in Molly's defense in court due to his area of specialization in the field. Patrick majors in defending abuse on the poor, displaced persons, and less privileged. This narrows his career down to the duties of human right activist.

"I will give it a try and see how it goes," she thought. She gently removed her arms from the car's roof on which she rested on and lethargically opened her purse to bring out her car key.

Instantly, she felt a touch on her shoulder accompanied by an unfamiliar voice.

"Hey"

"Hello, hi," she muttered as she turned shockingly.

"Sorry to startle you, I'm Felix but my friends call me Fex," he introduced himself smiling boldly as he stretched out his right hand for a handshake.

"Cool, I'm Margie," she replied with forced smiles as she fitted her right hand into his in return.

Margie tried as much as she could to control her in coordination because of the amount of shocks she has received for the day. "My blood pressure for this past few hours will definitely be high," she thought as she breathed in and out, pushing her shoulder up and down.

"Beautiful name," He praised and continued. "I came around to see my brother who was arrested for murder, he is an anesthetist. He got arrested for being part of a cloning trial that went wrong due to some medical complications that arose during the trial."

"So sorry, I came to see a friend too," she replied shallowly notwithstanding her friend's predicaments. With the mention of an anesthetist she figured out it is for Robin's case.

Suddenly, Fex's phone rings, she thought he would walk away and save her the long stand. Surprisingly, he ignored the call forcing Margie to speak up.

"Please take your call," she pleaded tranquilly.

"Don't mind that," he replied reluctantly and pushed his hands into his pockets to assume a better standing position for discussion.

"Ok," Margie replied making fastidious eye contacts showing discomfort. Unfortunately, considering her behavior isn't what Fex is out for.

"It shocks me how people can be so insensitive to another's emotions and welfare. The human subject that was used for the so called cloning trial died in the process of the trial. Unfortunately, he is an only son. His mother took to her stand to drag everyone involved in the trial to court because the medical consent was signed without her knowledge. Unimaginably, she approved the arrest of her own daughter too, can you believe that?"

"Yeah, it's on the news," Margie affirmed standing on her toes and falling back on her heels in discomposure.

"Good, what kind of a mother does that? She also went ahead to hire one of the..." he continued, pulling out his hands from his pockets to illustrate better.

"Can you just stop talking and let me go!" Margie acclaimed in her mind as she scratched her left ear frowning.

"Are you okay?" He slowly queried when he noticed Margie's gestures of discomfort.

"Yes, I am fine," she answered with unprecedented smiles.

"Cool, as I was saying," he continued as Margie looked up to the sky hopelessly. "She hired one of the most influential lawyers in Gozax against her own daughter, she…"

"Yeah, I think…" Margie interrupted immediately to cut the foreseen epistle. "She has the right to do whatever she wants; we keep praying she doesn't win." She added feeling clever enough to have maneuvered the situation.

"Cool, by the way. You look so lovely," he admired as he casts lustful stares and smiles on her.

"Thanks, please I have to run," she requested as she speedily opens her car.

"Can I at least get a hug or your phone number?" He begged hoping to get one of the two.

"No thanks," she said faintly as she entered and slammed the car's door. Margie's response froze him for some seconds, he least expected a snob from her.

"Arrogant bitch," he commented angrily and walked away.

"Hmmm," Margie breathed out as she watched him walk away from her side mirror and dropped her purse on the first passenger's seat. As she tried to insert the key into the ignition point and start the car she remembered Dorcas' works in a law firm as a psychologist and will be of great help to hire the best lawyer Molly needs.

Dorcas and Margie were compelled to become friends ever since their husbands started being friends and made the best out of it. Their friendship isn't so intimate because they don't share most things in common but never hesitates to help each other when called on.

"I think I should give her a call," Margie muttered as she

inserted the car key into the ignition point. She grabbed her purse, unzipped it and brought out her phone. Still holding unto the purse in her left hand, she pressed the separate button by the right side of her phone with her right thumb to on it.

"Wow," she acclaimed at the sight of the time which declared 2:36pm. Then she realized she spent almost three hours with Molly and Olivia. Although, the duration seemed brief but still quite long for a cell visitation. She quickly dialed Dorcas' number and placed the phone on her left ear hoping she will pick her call.

"Hey, good day," she greeted once Dorcas picked up.

"Good day, Mag," she replied, "How are you doing?" She quickly asked in a friendly tone.

"I'm fine dear, please are you still at work?" Margie speedily inquired to cut the exchange of pleasantries short.

"Yes, hope there's no problem?" Dorcas questioned. "Not at all," Margie answered shaking her head sideways in disagreement and continued, "I will be with you in few minutes, when is your closing hour?"

"5pm," she replied. "Ok I'm coming," Margie said as she quickly dropped the purse on her left hand where it was and turned on the ignition.

"Alright, I'm expecting you," Dorcas concluded as Margie hung up.

Her left hand handled the steering wheel while she dropped the phone on the same place it was with her right hand. She pulled out of the parking lot and drove out of the police station hurriedly.

She made a left turn into Mamieu-Beet when she casted a quick glance on the fuel gauge. "Shit!" she exclaimed with a frowning face denoting she is running out of fuel. It came to her mind that there are no fueling stations in the streets which entails she will have to go back to Barbie road which is a major road to buy fuel.

She hastily took the next chanced left turn into the other lane and drove back to Barbie road.

Margie pulled in her car into the least populated fueling station she saw and queued on the line awaiting her turn. As the line keeps moving sluggishly, she pulled out her head from the window and discovered it will still take time to get to her turn.

She comfortably brought her head into the car and unzipped her purse. Surprisingly, she found her earpiece in her purse and happily launched the speakers into her ears, turned on one of the music in her playlist and inserted the pointed pin in the earpiece into her phone's earpiece point and listened to it, nodding freely to its beats.

As the line kept moving, a young lad suddenly walked up to her and greeted her. But wasn't noticed due to the ear piece conveying a music she is wearing.

"Good day," he greeted again patting Margie on the shoulder.

"Hey," she replied as she realizes herself and pulled out the earpiece's speaker on her left ear.

"Sorry I was carried away by the music," she apologized humbly.

"Ok, I'm Peter," he introduced himself and stretched out his right hand for a handshake.

"Nice to meet you Peter, I'm Margie," she responded as they shook hands.

"I so much admired your beauty from my car over there and I decided to come and familiarize myself with this damsel radiating so much prettiness," he flattered. "Can I get your phone number so that I can call and know you…"

"Hey dude, let the lady be and come fill your fuel tank," the concerned individual said in a high tone.

"Oh," he said as he turned to the direction of his car, turned back to Margie and said, "Please, I will be right back."

"Ok," she agreed smiling friskily as he rushed back to his car. Margie shook her head sideways as she laughed for what just happened. She filled her fuel tank and drove off immediately not minding if he was waiting or not.

CHAPTER TWELVE

Black...?

The harsh entrance she made into *Absolute Justice Firm* immobilized the doorman and walked straight to the receptionist reluctantly not minding who was watching.

"Good afternoon ma, how may I help you?" The receptionist requested with a soft voice tone and smile.

"Please I want to see Dorcas, Yeah Dorcas Smith?" She answered spitefully neglecting the nice voice and smile.

"Do you have an appointment?" The receptionist questioned as she went through her computer.

"Yes, she knows I'm coming," Margie confirmed as the receptionist picked up the intercom caller to put a call through to Dorcas' office.

"Your name please?" The

receptionist inquired as she placed it on her right ear.

"Margie," she answered impatiently.

"Margie who?" The receptionist asked again irritating Margie.

"Please tell her Margie is here to see her, she will understand," Margie replied starkly with a high tone.

"Ok ma, please a young lady by name Margie is here to see you," the receptionist said as she heard Dorcas' voice.

"Please send her in" Dorcas permitted and ended the call.

"Ma, take the stairs up, the first office by your right on the first corridor," the receptionist guided.

"Thank you," Margie said meanly as she made her way to the stairs.

"Hello," Margie greeted as she opened and peeped into Dorcas's office smiling."Please come in,"

Dorcas said as she stood up to welcome her.

"Good to see you again after such a long time," she added as Margie shot the door.

"Really, has it been long?" Margie asked as they hugged each other and separated. "Yes of course, like 5 months now," she countered and noticed Margie still casts the doubt looks on her.

"Come on, we saw last after Charles's birthday," she explained further.

"I'm sorry I already forgot that," Margie apologized.

"Please have a seat," Dorcas offered pointing to the client's seat.

"Thank you," Margie appreciated as she sat down and dropped her purse and car key on Dorcas's desk. Dorcas walked back to her seat as she saw Margie sit.

"I do understand how busy we can be," Dorcas affirmed as they laughed. "You are not looking bad you know, Charles is really taking good care of you," she added smiling good-humoredly, turning her chair gradually sideways.

"For Christ's sake what's going on? You are the fourth person to accord that I'm beautiful today," Margie said as Dorcas laughed hard. "So unfortunate that I'm not seeing it," Margie lamented. "I understand; you don't need to see it. But you are glowing girl," Dorcas confirmed amidst smiles.

"Ok, thank you," Margie gave in shyly as she leaned back on the seat. "How is Shirley?" She asked interestedly. "I miss her small mouth," she added as they laughed.

"Shirley is fine, and Charles?" Dorcas questioned.

"He is glowing like me," she answered and they laughed again.

After a brief discussion on how their families are faring.

Margie quickly announced why she came.

"Uhmm, I'm here because of Molly."

"Oh, it's true. I saw it in the news this morning," Dorcas said, paused for a while as Margie nodded unhappily and she drew her seat closer to her desk to make a committed statement. "Indeed, so far our hearts still beat and our eyes still blinks, wonders will never cease to happen," she added miserably

"Yeah, that's why I'm here to seek for your help in hiring a good lawyer that can combat Vanessa confidently," Margie stated with so much seriousness that Dorcas had to stop what she was doing.

"Ok, I will," she accepted. "That wouldn't be a big deal, so do you have anyone in mind?" She inquired as she leaned back on her seat

"Yeah, I was thinking of Patrick Bee, but his specialization makes me doubt if he will stand in for Molly," Margie answered placing her left arm on the desk

"Asides that, Patrick is not in town." Dorcas revealed. "Wow," Margie chipped in. "Yeah, most lawyers are out of town for one of their conferences in Stockazul Island," she added.

"But Vanessa is in town?"Margie hurriedly asked inquisitively.

"Yeah, stories have it that she has some controversial scores to settle with them that's why she didn't go," she explained.

"I see," Margie asserted as Dorcas swiftly sat up on her seat.

"But I know a good one who can handle Molly's case," she assured.

"Really, who's that?" Margie asked interestedly.

"Ginika Emechelu," she answered smiling.

"Gini what? What's that?" Margie asked again in confusion.

"Ginika Emechelu," Dorcas repeated, "She is black."

"Black?" Margie questioned as she lay back on her seat frowning in disappointment. "What's wrong with it?" Dorcas asked immediately, fixing an intent gaze on her.

"Dorcas I need a capable lawyer who can stand Vanessa and not some black creature trying to fit in," Margie stressed on her opinion aggressively.

"Margie really, so you think her complexion and race makes her incapable?" Dorcas asked but got no reply.

"You really need to shake that mindset off your being," Dorcas cautioned because she least expected such response from Margie. "As far as I know and from experience of working with her, she is one of the best here and a readily available one to handle this case," Margie advised meanly.

"She should be in the conference right?" Margie smartly asked.

"Yes," Dorcas sluggishly replied as she held up the pen in her right hand, turning it vigorously.

"So?" Margie said but got no response. "Dorcas, all I am doing is for Molly. I can't imagine the worse befall her on this, that's why I'm being so sensitive about getting a skilled lawyer."

"Trust me Ginika is capable of whatever you want in that law court," Dorcas assured pointing to her left as if the law court was there.

"Alright, I will think about it and get back to you tomorrow morning," Margie requested.

"Ok, that's okay." She concluded. "I think I will go sign out and we go together," she concluded.

"But it's not yet time?" Margie quickly reminded.

"Yes, the dismissal time is 4pm. I extended the time so you can get here and also have enough time to discuss," she answered smiling as she stood up to get her bag.

"Really, thank you so much," Margie uttered happily as she stood up and collected her purse and car key.

"You are welcome," Dorcas replied picking her things one after the other.

Dorcas carefully zipped her handbag after putting all she came to work with. As she collected her bag to leave with Margie, she remembered the computer on her desk is still on. She quickly took a step backwards and bent her waist slightly to align her eyes with the computer. She kept casting hasty glances at each tab that pops up, following the due process diligently, until she shut it down.

"Let's go please," she said as she turned to Margie.

"Okay," Margie agreed and walked towards the door but noticed at some point that Dorcas wasn't coming after her, she quickly turned to know what must have drawn her back and discovered she wanted to pull the window's curtain to the other side in an enclosed form. She patiently waited as Dorcas battled with the curtain.

Dorcas still made her way to the right side of the wall where the air conditioner stood to switch it off as Margie slowly drew backwards towards the door and held its handle.

Margie quickly opened the door as soon as Dorcas switched off the air conditioner. The door's hinges made some noise sequel to Dorcas's pointed heels sounds as she walked towards the door. The hinges sound ceased as soon as the door got to its stop point by the right. Margie stepped out and stood on the

corridor as Dorcas cautiously placed her right hand on the bulb's switch by the right side of the door's frame and switched it off.

The office became so dark that one could hardly pin point anything in it. The office equipments stood still humbly, awaiting Dorcas's return for work in the morning.

Dorcas held the door's handle and drew the door to the left, making the door's lock to face her directly. She diligently pushed in the key into the lock and turned it to the right to make sound confirming that it has locked. She pulled out the key, unzipped her side bag to put the key and turned as Margie progressed to the stairs.

"I think I have to change the brand of heels I wear," Dorcas asserted as she held the stairs reel and carefully watched her steps through the stair in order not to fall.

"Which one do you patronize?" Margie asked interestedly as she looked back at her to ascertain if the brand is a good one or not.

"Shy brand," she replied and stopped on the plain ground before the next stairs prompting Margie to stop too.

"Shy?" Margie ascertained surprisingly expecting no response as she turned back to face her. "I wear Shy brands too," she added as she held unto the reel with her left hand and placed her right hand with which she held her purse on her waist, making her left knee joint to bend backwardly to compensate the standing position.

"It hurts the back side of my ankle," Dorcas complained as she slants her right leg to the left to enable Margie see the already healing wound she incurred from one of her heels. Margie bent down a little to see the wound "This may be caused by extremely tight heeled shoe's edges," Margie assured as she stood erect.

"Definitely, my shoes are tight on me but not extremely tight. Despite that, I still get these irritating wounds," she complained sadly.

"Anyway" Margie said as she turned to continue walking down the stairs. "I wear Shy brands too but don't get such wounds," she added and stopped again to make a point.. "I advise you change them and watch out for outcomes of other brands and try to avoid tight shoes. Instead, buy loose shoes and add tissue paper at the toe point to make up for the remaining length," she recommended keenly and continued walking down the stairs.

"Okay," Dorcas accepted willingly.

When they got to the reception, Margie recalled her ordeal with the receptionist and casted a friendly smile at her to reimburse for the unfavorable encounter she had with her. The receptionist understood what her smiles meant and waved at her to buttress a friend zone between them.

"This way," Margie directed pointing to Charles's car as they stepped out of the firm.

"Charles's car must have performed a whole lot of work today," Dorcas said as they laughed and walked down to the spot Margie parked the car. "It has taken me to countless places today. Thank God for technology," Margie confirmed as she opened the car's doors with its remote.

"I can imagine how tough the day has been for the helpless car," Dorcas teased.

"Yeah," Margie affirmed as they both entered the car at the same time.

Margie started the car and kept looking backward through the back glass to enable her see what is behind her. She pulled out of the parking lot carefully, managing the limited space the firm has to turn and drive out.

The common challenge most workers in Tokex has is

morning and evening hours' traffic jams. By the time Margie drove out of the firm, the streets were already congested.

The evening rush of the streets and major roads was already at its peak. The pedestrian lane is overwhelmed with thousands of people on it. Each passer-by wouldn't mind pushing down its counterpart to get to its destination.

The road side sellers contribute greatly to this jam because of their routine evening business transactions with their customers which drastically slows down the movement frequency on the roads.

The government efficiently in situated traffic lights on major roads, busy streets and junctions to enforce smooth movements on the road during morning and evening hours. The present government also progressively provided robots that that ensures order by signaling traffic commands during these busy hours.

The robots and traffic signs are never found incompetent or malfunctioning, but the road congestions always render them invisible. Over time, Gozax's advancement in technology has devised a means of using the kinetic energy produced by the friction of the foot wares and vehicle tires that pass on busy roads during these hectic hours to generate electricity.

Car horns keeps blowing, high vocal tantrums stroke at any end it can reach and unmanaged movements of the pedestrians kept the street on a motion of chaos.

Margie had gotten used to the streets and kept maneuvering junctions with traffic congestions. Unfortunately, she got to Alumzy junction which leads to Mamieu-Green where Dorcas resides and couldn't help but join the queue.

"You are indeed good in this," Dorcas confessed. "I can't believe we are here already," she declared as she kept staring around in amazement.

"Thank you, I will negotiate with Charles to establish a driving school," Margie chipped in playfully as they laughed. "Exactly," Dorcas affirmed amidst laughter.

"Wow," she declared with her eyes wide open glittering with enormous anxiety when Margie quickly matched on the brake to stop the car from moving as she nearly hit a stranger. If not for Dorcas's seat belt she would have hit her head on the car's air vent due to the force at which the car stopped.

"What's wrong?" She asked curiously breathing hard.

"I nearly hit that man," Margie reported pointing at the man, who stood still in front of the car, checking himself to ensure he had no scratch. "But he was on my way," Margie defended as she turned to Dorcas breathing hard too.

"Oh my God; he is coming to your window," Dorcas asserted in fear as Margie quickly winded up her window's glass to a level the man wouldn't reach her. As he got closer he displayed aggressive moves with incomprehensive language.

CHAPTER THIRTEEN

Spanish challenge

Dorcas shivered in fear as he drew closer, her breathing pace kept increasing as his steps with fury emerged. Margie wasn't scared as much as she was ready for the worse with him. She previously has had encounters with people of this sort in traffic jams and was ready to have him deliver his worse.

"Margie, please pull up your window's glass completely please, I can't stand this man hurting you please," Dorcas pleaded with a shaking voice but got no response from Margie."Oh God, oh God!" Dorcas added and closed her eyes, holding her hands together underneath her jaw as the young man knocked on Margie's window's glass.

Margie adjusted on her seat to enable him see half of her face, her eyes precisely. Although, she pretended to be in control of the situation, her tensed eyes still radiated fear of the young man's masculinity.

"Hi," she said maintaining eye contact with him.

"Que sertu el problema la nina?" He said angrily to Margie's confusion as Dorcas quickly opened her eyes.

"Que what?" Margie replied.

"I think he is speaking Spanish," Dorcas intervened humbly. "Cool, because I don't understand anything," Margie retorted as the young man kept talking to himself in a high tone, increasing his anger.

"Young man, I do not understand you," Margie shouted back aggressively casting hateful looks on him. "Hey, it's okay," Dorcas asserted to calm Margie down, drew closer to Margie and raised her face to create an eye contact with the young man.

"Holla!" She waved to the man but was ignored as he continued barking at Margie.

"Est artuci ego? Que tu no poderver mi?" He said as he pointed his left fingers at the front of the car angrily. "Thank God I do not understand you," Margie said carelessly.

Margie's nonchalant response prompted Dorcas to intervene again.

"Lo sentimos, por favor perdone a mi amigo," Dorcas pleaded meekly on Margie's behalf establishing a bridge over the language barrier between the two parties. Although, he understood Dorcas he still raged restlessly due to Margie's first reaction.

"En lugar de lamenter que levanto la voz sobre mi," he complained furiously pointing at Margie as she looked away. "Por favor perdona nos," Dorcas pleaded again calmly with her hands joined together.

"Let's get out of here please," Margie chipped in indifferently as she tried to move but was stopped by Dorcas. "Can you just behave?" Dorcas cautioned looking intently at her as the man kept expressing his resentment. "He was on my way, what am I supposed to do?" Margie questioned raising her shoulder and eyebrows.

As the traffic's queue kept moving, Margie didn't move to enable Dorcas settle with the man. Other drivers behind Margie began horning with their cars as they waited for Margie to move but she didn't.

"You know you owe him an apology right?" Dorcas queried meanly. "Unfortunately, I don't understand him," Margie defended herself strongly as Dorcas ignored her reason to talk with the man.

"Por favor," Dorcas still pleaded as she noticed his anger subsidizing. "Tienes mucha suerte," he stated with an odious gaze on Margie and walked away unexpectedly. "Gratias," Dorcas shouted to his hearing as he walked away, leaned back on her seat and Margie drove forward

"So, now drivers behind me will render me deaf with their loud horns because of some ill-mannered Spanish guy," she uttered carelessly as she matched the brake at the back of the next car.

"They should wait, Margie," Dorcas said meanly. "I'm sure you don't want to incur the wrath of these aggressive drivers," Margie uttered as she lifts her hands off the steering wheel.

"Whatever, you don't just treat people like that," she added. "I couldn't comprehend what he was saying, if not for you…" Margie defended herself strongly again.

"Those reasons are irrelevant, courtesy demands you wait and apologize. Even if you don't understand each other, use signs," Dorcas advised and looked away angrily. "Thanks for that Mrs. Psychologist," Margie teased and laughed.

The traffic congestion kept moving until Margie was privileged to make a right turn into Mamieu-Beet.

"Thank goodness we are here. By the way, when did you learn Spanish, such that you could speak it so fluently?" Margie asked curiously throwing glances at Dorcas and driving at the same time.

"I was privileged to be in Madrid for my master's degree under Absolute Justice. That was before I met Tom," Dorcas smiled proudly. "Wow! That's good. At least you are diversified in lingual perspective," Margie complimented as she nodded appreciatively. "So, can you translate what you guys discussed please," she requested calmly and still maintained a deranged glance on the road.

"Okay. First when he came to your window he asked, 'what is your problem young girl?' Dorcas explained illustratively. "Ouch! Young girl? Does he even know I'm married?" Margie questioned sadly, "I don't know," Dorcas replied with laughter and continued.

"He also asked if you are blind that you didn't see him."

"OK, that must be when he pointed at the front of the car," she affirmed. "Yeah, then I said 'Hello, we are sorry, please forgive my friend. And he complained that instead of saying sorry, you shouted at him." Dorcas explained plainly. "Really?" Margie exclaimed with her eyes and mouth wide open.

"Yeah, I still pleaded and he said you are so lucky and walked away angrily" Dorcas continued explaining.

"Me? What exactly can he do?" Margie challenged arrogantly. "You never can tell," Dorcas chipped in raising her shoulders "Well, I concluded with Thank you," she added.

"Please I know Gracias means thank you," Margie boosted as they laughed. "You need to pay me for saving your ass out there," Dorcas teased as she opened her left palm in request for the money. "Really, I must sign up for a Spanish language class then," Margie retorted as they laughed.

As Margie pulled into Dorcas' residence, Shirley rushed out of the house to report how her day went.

"Welcome mummy," she greeted as they hugged each other.

"Thank you dear. How was your…" Dorcas inquired when Shirley caught sight of Margie and quickly left her arms and rushed into Margie's.

"How are you my love?" Margie asked smiling.

"I'm good, Uncle Charles was here and he promised me a bronze bangle the next time he comes," Shirley reported happily.

"A bronze bangle?" Dorcas and Margie asked simultaneously and looked at each other with surprise.

"Yes, he said bronze bangles are believed to be special and it attracts good lucks," she explained happily, laughing clearly, to expose her incomplete incisors.

"Interesting," Margie commented smiling mischievously and looked away.

"That must be kind of Uncle Charles," Dorcas stated in Charles's favor. "The Rosary man also promised me a rosary," Shirley said as they proceeded for the balcony. "Yeah, you told me. What about that?" Dorcas asked interestedly as they walked side by side.

"Rosary man, who's that?" Margie asked inquisitively.

"That's Mr. Douglas," Dorcas replied in a low tone. "Oh," Margie said as she sat down on one of the chairs on the balcony. "Good evening Tom," Margie greeted as Tom stepped out of the house.

"Good evening Margie, how are you?" He asked smiling boldly. "Good evening love," Dorcas greeted with attractive smiles. "Good evening dear," he responded as they hugged.

"How is your day going?" He inquired as they loosed hold of each other. "My day is going fine, and Margie made my evening," she answered smiling at Margie and she smiled back.

"That's good," he concluded as Shirley jumped on his laps. "Easy baby," he advised as he placed her on his laps.

"As I was saying, I went to the Rosary man's house to get the rosary he promised me but he wasn't around," Shirley carped with a soft tender voice. "Also, Chizzy said her mom told her Rosary man was arrested in the church this morning. Is that true?" she asked curiously as she stared at each of them for an answer.

"Yes dear," Tom spoke up."Really!" Shirley exclaimed with her eyes wide open radiating with so much astonishment. "And that's all I know," Tom added smartly to

avoid further critical questions as they laughed.

"I think I should be going," Margie quickly said as she stood up to leave.

"Don't go, you haven't had anything," Dorcas pleaded with so much concern.

"Aunty Mag, daddy made a delicious dinner, please join us," Shirley revealed with a puffed up cheeks as she went close to Margie and dragged her hand to persuade her into staying.

"Really, that's generous of you," Dorcas said happily patting his back.

"You are welcome," he said smiling at her. "At least have dinner with us," Tom added to convince Margie to stay. "I'm sorry I really need to run; Charles must be waiting," she stated calmly as she touched Shirley's cheeks.

"I will definitely mobilize your special bangles majestically," she promised with fabricated walking styles to show how the bangle will be delivered, smiling simultaneously.

"Okay," Shirley accepted smiling boldly.

"Thanks for the ride dear, my regards to Charles," Dorcas said as Margie stood below the entrance stairs.

"Sure, you are welcome, bye," she said waving at them and headed for her car.

They watched her leave and waved their hands to bid a goodbye.

"Today was really hectic. Thanks baby for dinner," Dorcas stated thankfully with smiles as Shirley jumped on Tom's back. "You are welcome dear," he managed to say faintly as he bent to enable Shirley relax on his back.

Dorcas made her way back to where she sat to carry her handbag. Just then she felt the pains of her heels again.

"Ouch!" she asserted and hurriedly sat down, frowning her face in pains. "What's

wrong?" Tom quickly asked and drew closer to her to ascertain what the problem is. Almost simultaneously, Shirley popped up her head from Tom's left shoulder and asked intently, "Mom are you okay?"

"Yes dear, my heel hurts," she answered in pains still frowning, as she pulled off her heels. "Let me see?" Tom requested as he bent down to enable him see it, making Shirley to draw forward sharply. "Dad!" Shirley quickly shouted in fear of falling. "Hold on tight dear," Tom cautioned as he stood erect to enable her encircle her hands round his neck, and bent down again.

"Sorry mummy," Shirley said softly. "Thanks dear," she muttered with pain in a low tone.

"I think you should change them then," Tom advised as he grabbed her right ankle. "Margie advised same. I will do that as soon as possible because this really hurts," Dorcas said gloomily as she caressed her legs.

"Sorry dear," Tom commiserated softly. "Come on Shirley, let's sprinkle the breeze of healing," Tom summoned as they hastily bent over, narrowed their cheeks, to tilt their lips forward and enable cool air pass through.

"How do you feel now?" Tom asked as Shirley jumped down from his back. "Better," Dorcas managed to say to please them. "Indeed, the healing breeze does wonders," she forcefully added amidst pains and smiles.

"Yes!" Tom and Shirley acclaimed and clapped their hands in the air. "I wish it's so," Dorcas muttered as she glared at them. "You said?" Shirley questioned intently thinking she still needs the healing breeze as Tom looked at her curiously to know why she murmured. "Nothing dear," she assured.

"Good," Shirley declared and smiled back. "Please the next breeze I want to feel is dinner, I'm famished," Dorcas alleged as they laughed out loudly. "I expected that," Tom teased amidst laughter.

"Alright, I will get your shoes and bag", he added, bent down and collected them. Shirley quickly jumped down from the seat on which she sat and reminded, "Dad, remember we are the magnificent ushers."

"Oh!" Tom acclaimed with his eyes wide open. "I almost forgot," he added and hit his head with his left hand regrettably. "Thanks for that…"

"Magnificent ushers? What's that?" Dorcas interrupted curiously amidst intense confusion, as she stared at them. "Relax baby and enjoy the royal welcome," Tom retorted with a bold smile that revealed his upper gums.

"Okay," she accepted with smiles too awaiting the huge surprise.

"Mmmm," Tom quickly cleared his throat impishly as he put her heels on his left hand with which he held the handbag and hastily angled his elbow for Dorcas to hold on to.

CHAPTER FOURTEEN

Here comes the queen

As she stood up and gripped her left hand to his arm, Shirley rushed forward and stood still with fascinating smiles, holding her hands together at the center of her stomach. Tom manipulatively raised his baritone voice as he ordered the majestic train loudly .

"Shoulders high…Head upright…Chest out. Here comes the Queen of the Smith's empire."

"*Here comes the Queen,*

Here comes the Queen,

Here comes the queen of the Smith's empire." Shirley sang with her tiny voice as they majestically matched into the house.

Dorcas held her mouth with her right hand in order not to let out the laughter which she was concealing. Concurrently, she felt honored. Although, the entrance was performed with so much unscrupulous skills, she felt like a queen indeed.

On getting to the sitting room, Shirley swiftly turned in order to create a path for them to pass through, standing at attention, with her joint hands still at the same position.

They slowly walked to the cushion. Tom quickly dropped the shoes and bag, held her hand in a bent position to help her have her seat.

Instantly, Shirley sharply moved to her left hand side as Tom positioned himself on the right. They stamped their right foots concomitantly and chorused,

"Hail, Queen Dorcas of the Smith's empire!"

Dorcas couldn't hold back her laughter and they all joined her happily in the laughing session.

"But, be sincere, how do you feel?" Tom asked interestedly when he finally controlled his

laughter. "Well, I feel…" Dorcas tried to express herself but lacked the right words to use. "I feel privileged, loved and esteemed. You are the best," she concluded, pecked Shirley's forehead and kissed Tom passionately.

"Yes! We did it!" Shirley acclaimed as Tom and Dorcas separated from each other. "Yeah," Tom supported smiling.

"Mom, you needed to see the series of practices and efforts it took to perfect this," Shirley detailed with bold smirks. "Really, I'm super proud of you dear," Dorcas asserted unpretentiously and hugged her passionately.

"I wish I recorded this with my phone, I will brag about with it wherever I go," she added almost in tears, "You are the best," she complimented as she hugged Tom, while Shirley rushed and held them.

"We love you, mom," Shirley said in a low tone almost inaudible.

"I love you too," Dorcas replied as Tom kissed her forehead.

As they let go of themselves, the hunger stings struck Dorcas's abdominal walls again.

"Please I have to go and freshen up for dinner," she pleaded frowning as Tom and Shirley sat down on the cushion. "Because right now, I'm starving," she added holding her stomach with her hands.

"Oh now, you are starving," Tom teased with laughter and clung his right hand over Shirley's shoulder.

"Mom, please go. We will be right here," Shirley assured. "That's my baby," Dorcas said cheerfully, walked up to Shirley, pecked her right, and left cheek sequentially.

Instantly, Tom quickly grabbed the remote on the center table to change the channel.

"Daddy," Shirley screamed with gritted teeth as Dorcas headed for the room. "What!" He questioned with a strange look full of surprise and sat down. Shirley hastily knelt down on the cushion, placed her hands together uprightly, closed her eyes a bit and appealed in a low tone "Nickelodeon please."

"Oh that…no way," Tom asserted meanly as he leaned back on the cushion, grasped the pillow to his chest and looked into the remote to locate the channel number he wants. Shirley quickly drew closer and gripped his right elbow.

"Dad, please channel 37, channel 37, 37, 37 please 37…" she kept whispering to him with a depressed face. "You know I don't watch that," Tom asserted to Shirley's bewilderment. She swiftly removed her hands from his elbow to face him directly.

"No, that's not true," she argued as she folded her arms underneath her chest, grimacing. "We always watch Nickelodeon together, every day, right here, in this sitting room," she detailed, pointing with her right hand to the television and the sitting room to show how they do it.

"Really?" Tom asked pretentiously in confusion. "Yes," Shirley responded boldly, looking at him intently to ascertain his next excuse. "Maybe, that was then. But right now, I want to watch the news," he said meanly and fixed his gaze on the television as he pressed the channel number he wanted.

Shirley suddenly became gloomy and conceitedly assumed a crying mood. "Dad, please don't do this to me," she pleaded with a shivering voice as she held onto his right elbow again and lowered her forehead on it. "Please..." she pleaded again to make Tom change his decision.

"Ok... Nickelodeon," he succumbed meekly to her plea. "Wow, thanks daddy. You are the best," she said happily as she hugged him. "Yeah, anything for you dear," Tom concluded and pecked her forehead.

"Now Nickelodeon," he added as he pressed 37 on the remote and Shirley sat close to him with obvious happiness all over her face.

As the channel took a while to show up, Shirley remembered how lucky she was to have Tom and Dorcas.

"Dad," she called softly. "Yes dear," he answered calmly as he turned to her. "Guess my prayer intentions whenever we pray the rosary with the rosary man," she demanded fixing an intent gaze on his face. "What?" H questioned interestedly as he couldn't lay his hands on what exactly her prayer intentions were.

"Firstly, I usually thank God for making you and mom my parents," she replied smiling.

"Really?" Tom ascertained as he withdrew his shoulders to the right a bit in amazement, to be sure she actually said that.

"Yes, because I know most of my classmates whose parents are divorced and what they pass through," she retorted with solemnity as Tom nods sadly, feeling for those children she talked about.

"Secondly, I always pray you and mom will remain together. Thirdly, God should bless me with a baby sister," she stated emotionally. "Come here," Tom said in a low tone, drew her closer and hugged her tightly such that her head is almost invisible. Then, he held her shoulders.

"Look at me," he said as Shirley raised her eyes to his. "Thank God for me and your mummy, Thank God for you. You are more than a blessing to us," he asserted looking intently at her. "I give you my word, me and mom will never file a divorce. Even if we do, God with his special grace will

not allow that, for your sake," he assured passionately as Shirley nods in agreement and they hugged each other again.

"I love you so much my angel," Tom whispered to her ear. "I love you too daddy," she replied softly. "And you will surely have a baby sister very soon," Tom assured again as they unglued from each other. "Really, thank you," she appreciated and pounced on him joyfully.

Dorcas emerged as they let go of each other.

"What's going on here?" She inquired curiously as she looked at them suspiciously. "I was telling dad of my prayer intentions when we pray the rosary with the rosary man," Shirley answered calmly.

"Interesting, I guess they are not bad ones?" Dorcas inquired as she drew Shirley to herself. "Yes," she responded with smiles. "Good," Dorcas said, knelt down in front of Shirley and slowly closed her eyes. "To all of my baby's prayer intentions, I pray you oh Lord to grant awesomely, in Jesus name," she prayed and Tom and Shirley chorused. "Amen."

"I love you so much, mummy," Shirley said and hugged her. "I love you more dear," Dorcas whispered softly as they still held each other.

"Enough of the love, dinner please," Tom quickly interrupted as he couldn't bear the hunger any longer. "That's true," Dorcas affirmed as she unexpectedly carried Shirley up.

"Mum," she called out joyfully.

"What? You think you have outgrown my arms?" She asked with an interrogative gaze as they all laughed and progressed to the dining.

Dorcas placed Shirley on the first seat by the left and made her way to the right. "Thank you, mummy," Shirley said appreciatively, leering as she adjusted on her seat. "Thank

you too baby," Dorcas replied as she sat down on her seat.

"For what?" She asked inquisitively. "For being my baby," Dorcas replied with bold smiles as Shirley smiled back.

Tom drew out his seat from the head of the table, in between them and sat down. "Dishing time!" Dorcas acclaimed. "Salivating time!" Shirley responded as they laughed.

"No…no, let me do that. I did the cooking remember?" Tom said interrupting their laughter. "Oh," Dorcas affirmed raising her eyebrows and handed over the ladle to him. "Have your way my sweet chef," she said sneering at him.

The dishing time is indeed the salivating time in the Smith's residence. As Tom dished the food so did Dorcas and Shirley's taste buds agitate for the delicious meal, they swallowed tons of saliva and inhaled enough aroma from the food before Tom finished dishing it. He kept smiling with so much pride as he watched their expressions. Dorcas quickly prayed over the meal and they launched their forks into the pasta.

"Dad, you are indeed a great cook. I mean, this tastes good," Shirley praised with attractive smiles. "Thanks baby," he accepted favorably as he caressed her right cheek. "Not just good, my dear. He is exceptional," Dorcas confirmed as she chewed the pasta in her mouth.

"I have always witnessed his cooking skills on rare occasions. So, whenever daddy cooks, it's always special to me," She smacked her lips with delight over Tom's cooking skills. "Thanks love, you praise me too much, this is just pasta," he asserted raising his shoulder.

"This is more than a Pasta, dad," Shirley chipped in as she quickly swallowed the last portion of chewed pasta in her mouth. "Yeah," Dorcas affirmed as she looked at him

zealously. "Alright, I see it as a privilege whenever I do this. So, it's nothing," he assured as he gathered a portion of pasta with his fork.

"We love you dear," Dorcas affirmed as he cuddled his right elbow. "Hmmm, like you have an option?" He teased as he looked at them weirdly and they laughed.

When the laughter ceased, Tom quickly guessed why Margie visited.

"I suppose Margie came for Molly's case," he asked looking intently at his wife. "Yeah, she came so that I can help her arrange a capable lawyer to stand in for Molly," she affirmed and pushed some portion of her hair behind her left ear. "That's good," Tom affirmed as he chewed his food.

"I recommended Ginika Emechelu," Dorcas said pointing her empty fork from one direction to another. "Wow, that's good," Tom affirmed. "Yeah, but Margie seems not to be at home with it," she reported frowning. "Why? Ginika is amazing," he asked with dimmed eyes full of disappointment.

"Because she is black," she answered as she slowly poured some water from the jug into her cup. "What? I hope she is ready to get Molly a good lawyer," Tom asked interestedly. "Please I need some water too," he requested. "Okay," Dorcas responded as she positioned his cup and poured in water almost to its brim.

"I explained a lot to her, I believe she will come around," Dorcas assured as she handed over the cup of water to him.

Margie got home very tired as she had to fight through another traffic to get to her residence.

The car's door sounded too hard as she slammed it. She sluggishly numbered her steps to the entrance door, dragging her purse along with her right

index finger as if it is too heavy for her to carry.

She rested on the door's left frame, managed to place her right hand on the car's handle, dragged it downwards weakly and slowly pushed the door inside to create enough space for her to pass through. As she entered she breathed out heavily, showing a sign of relief.

She held the inside door handle and shot the door behind her. Wishes kept streaming into her head as she leaned on the door, closed her eyes tightly and slowly removed each of her shoes with the help of each leg.

With her eyes closed she imagined a helping hand could carry her to the room, bath her, feed her and do all she needed to do for herself before she goes to bed. But all varnished as she heard Charles call her name.

"Wow…you are back?" He asked as he drew closer to her. "Yes dear," she answered weakly with cloudy eyes. He noticed Margie's strange attitude and weakness as she bent down and gripped her shoes with her middle two left finger. "Is everything alright?"

"Yes dear, I'm tired," she responded and fell on him faintly.

He grabbed her. "Woo, be careful," he advised as he waved her hair from her face to see how exhausted she really is. As Margie didn't say any other word to him, he quickly carried her up like a baby and headed to the room.

He enabled her pull off her clothes and she took her bath. Margie walked out of the bathroom refreshed. She did expect her sweet husband to help her in every way he can. She walked up to him and hugged him from behind the reading chair he sat on.

"Ouch, you are cold," he declared as he leaned away to abstain from feeling her body temperature. "I just took my bath, what do you expect?" She asked rhetorically with

smiles as she sat on the table on which Charles is working on.

"How do you feel?" He asked as he grasped her wrists. "I feel…anew, fresh…" she said smiling. "I can see that," He affirmed.

"Please quickly change let's have dinner," Charles advised. "I guess you must be hungry," he added. "Very hungry," she confirmed as she tightened the towel she wrapped round her chest "By the way, you prepared dinner?" She asked immediately as she held up his face.

"Yes dear," he replied leering as he held her waist. "That's thoughtful of you dear," she complimented as she caressed his head. "I will quickly…" she tried to say but was interrupted as she caught sight of the heading on Charles's computer.

"Oh my God!" She screamed with delight. "The Atlanta Estate Wi-Fi project?" She asked with her eyes wide open as she turned to Charles in amazement. "Yes dear," he replied smiling. "You have it?"

"Not yet, the rich dude said he needs the survey…" he answered still smiling. "For?" Margie quickly interrupted inquisitively. "I don't know" he responded raising his shoulder and cheeks. "But on a 85 percent scale, we have the contract. He just needs to see our plan, that's all," he detailed further. "Wow, that's amazing,," Margie replied smiling as she danced round Charles's chair.

"That's good news," she confirmed as she placed her hands on his shoulder "Yeah, thank God for that," he concluded.

Margie walked to the wardrobe to change into her night wear.

"How is Molly? How is she coping with the new environment? Hope she is not feeling bad?"

"Wow, too many questions," Margie replied as she opened the wardrobe and continued, "Well, to your greatest surprise, Molly is more than fine."

"I don't understand," Charles expressed in a confused state. "Okay…she should be fine, but not totally in a police cell," he added as he adjusted to face Margie from the side.

"Yeah, I am fully aware of what I'm saying. Molly is doing great," she explained faintly as she stood on her toe to be able to remove her hanged night ware from its hanger. "How exactly?" Charles still asked in doubts.

"Let's say she encountered something stimulating and she has a company too," she answered as she closed the wardrobe.

"A company?" He questioned again, "Yeah, a friend kind of," she replied with smiles as she put her hands through the night wear. "Olivia, a little girl of eight years," she added. "Hmm, that's quite interesting," he chipped in as he adjusted on his seat again.

Margie slowly sat down on the bed, holding her wet towel. She kept caressing the towel while she selected the right words to express how strong Molly is.

"You know I expected her to be depressed and devastated," she said with a stern gaze on him. "But she showed the reverse. She was less emotional; she was consoling me instead when I cried for her," she explained "Really?"

"Yeah, I became encouraged by her. We had a nice time together. We sang Robin's favorite songs, discussed with them. We had a nice time," she detailed with smiles.

"Nice, I'm glad to hear that," he affirmed happily. "I also discussed with Dorcas to arrange a lawyer," she said as she stood up to hang her towel.

"That's good, how did it go?" He inquired as he stood up as well and leaned on the wall.

"She revealed that lawyers are on conference at Stockazul Island. With that, it will be quite stressful to get a lawyer that can defend her. So, she recommended one that works in her firm," Margie explained as she turned to him. "Who's that?"

"Ginika somebody, I can't really pronounce her surname. She is black and a good one," she stated frowning. "What?" Charles quickly asked as he noticed the strange face. "Black..." she answered still grimacing. "I doubt if she is capable," she added in a low tone, almost inaudible.

"Really, please get your mind off that. The blacks are really breaking limits recently...I know of a black guy that defended my boss for fraud and he performed well. If Dorcas recommends her, then she must have done that out of experience. Give it a try," he advised.

"Ok, I will call her tomorrow to give her a reply of

acceptance," she submitted meekly as they both sat down on the bed.

"But Vanessa should be in the conference too?" He asked curiously as he turned to her. "Yes, she has some issues to settle with the bar's association, that's why she is not there."

"I see," he said as he scratched his raised right eye brows.

After few seconds of silence, Margie remembered Charles's promise to Shirley and asked with smiles.

"What did you promise Shirley again?"

"Shirley?" he muttered as he tried to remember. "Oh! "A bronze bangle," he added as Margie boosts into laughter.

"Where do you intend to get that from?" she asked curiously amidst laughter. "I don't know," he answered raising his shoulder. "Maybe from one of the malls," he added inoffensively to justify

his means as Margie laughed harder.

"That will be tough dear," she advised as she tried to control her laughter. "I don't know how, but I will buy it."

"Better do because Shirley…hmm," she advised keenly as they burst into laughter for they know how persuasive Shirley can be and proceeded to the dining for dinner.

Very early the next day, St. Felix Catholic Church giant bell began ringing at exactly 5am prompt. It awoke Charles and every other Tokex's inhabitant that is sensitive to the bell.

As the bells kept on ringing to reach its maximum before stop, Charles gradually turned weakly to his left and blindly traced his phone on the bed lamp stand. He quickly opened his eyes dimly to grasp his phone as it nearly fell off his hand.

As the phone took its time to boot, he yawned carefully covering half of his mouth with his right wrist in order not to awake Margie.

He sat upright on the bed waiting for the phone to show up its apps. As soon as the phone was done with its preliminary booting procedure, its brightness ignited a significant light on Charles's face such that his head and face can be clearly seen even without the aid of an additional light source.

The phone's time displayed 05:02am.

He pressed the on-button once to put off its brightness. He swiftly opened the huge blanket which enveloped him and climbed down from the bed. He quietly opened the wardrobe and brought out his sports trouser where it hung. He gently dropped his phone on one of the wardrobes shelf, pulled off his night wear and hastily put on his trouser.

After putting on clothes, Charles walked back to the bed and sat on it, loosened the shoe laces one after the other. He gently slotted his legs into each of them and tightened the shoe lace to his fitting.

He slowly opened the last drawer in the bed lamp stand, collected his phone holder and clutched it to his right elbow. He inserted his earpiece into the phone, selected the first music on his playlist. He gently fixed the phone into the holder on his elbow and put one of the earpiece's speakers into his left ear.

Margie was fast asleep when he stepped out of the room. He left the house and locked it with his own key. With that he kicked off his morning joggling.

Margie was on call with Dorcas when he came back. He heard her voice as he stepped into the sitting room

"Babe?"

"Yes dear," she answered from the kitchen. "I'm here dear," she added covering the phone's speaker with her hand.

She hastily returned to the call as she noticed Charles is heading to the kitchen.

"I'm sorry, Charles just stepped in," she apologized as she released her hand from the speaker.

Margie slowly turned to him as he felt his embrace from the back. "I will be in your office during lunch hour so that we can meet her and negotiate the terms," she said with smiles and quickly pulled herself from him as he tickled her ribs.

"That's good, but can you come earlier than lunch time?" Dorcas inquired.

"That won't be feasible for me dear," she stated apologetically. "I absented from work yesterday because of Molly and taking an excuse today wouldn't be suitable."

"Okay, I understand," Dorcas said. She turned and saw Shirley emerging gradually from the kitchen with a tray of three tea cups. "Careful please," Dorcas advised keenly in a low tone as Shirley puffed up her cheeks to smile.

"Alright, I will schedule an appointment with her immediately," Dorcas assured as Shirley carefully placed the tray on the table and headed back to the kitchen. "An appointment? In the same work place?" Margie asked curiously as she opened the pancakes she had prepared for breakfast and Charles giggled silently.

"Yeah, we do that for security purposes. But, not to worry, since it's from a colleague it wouldn't be a difficult one," she explained as she held the phone firm to her ear with her shoulder to enable her place the mugs in its positions. "Wow, that's cool," Margie acknowledged as she carried the bowl of pancakes to the dining.

Suddenly, a disastrous sound is heard from Dorcas's side, making her to turn quickly to the direction of the sound. "Oh my God!" Dorcas screamed loudly to Margie's surprise as she dropped the phone on the dining table.

The sudden sound left Margie in a restless condition as Dorcas couldn't speak up to clarify her on what the problem is. She hurriedly dropped the table towel she had on the dining table and changed her phone to the other ear in confusion, to ascertain if she could hear something tangible.

Although, she hears unexamined voices from Dorcas's side, she still could lay her hands on what the tantrum is for.

"What happened?" She asked interestedly. She hastily beckoned on Dorcas as she got no reply. "Hello? Dorcas what is it?"

As Charles brought the tea cups to the dining table, he noticed Margie's strange look and asked inquiringly. "What's wrong?"

"I don't know, I heard an obvious sound, she screamed loudly after that and I can hear her cry from the back ground," Margie explained in confusion as she still beckoned. "Hello?" But got no reply.

"Who's that?" Charles questioned. "Dorcas," Margie replied frowning.

"Wow, that isn't ordinary, can I have the phone?" He requested as Margie handed the phone over to him humbly and glared at him agitatedly. "Hello?" Charles said audibly as he heard Tom's voice instantaneously.

"What's wrong?" Tom asked with his eyes wide open gleaming with curiosity. "What!" He shouted at the sight of Dorcas pulling Shirley up from the floor.

"Tom?" Charles called out but got no reply. "Hello, can someone tell us what's going on there?" He asked loudly but got no response as Margie paced about.

Tom quickly rushed to them to intervene. "What happened?" He asked Dorcas as he held Shirley up. "She fell with this jug of hot water," she answered almost in tears, pointing at the shattered jug. "What!" He acclaimed and quickly carried Shirley up to the dining.

He sat on one of the dining chairs and placed her on his laps judiciously. "Shirley?" He called as he looked into her eyes; his heart was beating abnormally fast.

"Daddy," she answered inaudibly in tears. "Yes dear, talk to me how do you feel?"

"Baby, please I think we should take her to the hospi…" Dorcas advised in fear as her hands shivered but was interrupted by Charles's voice which still called from the phone.

She snappily grabbed the phone and placed it on her ear. "Hello," she said as she paced about. "Hi, Dorcas," Charles replied with relief. "Is that Dorcas? What happened?" Margie questioned on hearing Dorcas's name as she returned from the kitchen, bearing a pen knife on her left hand.

She quickly sat down on her seat and fixed an unalterable gaze of concentration on him. "Why did you scream so loud? What happened?" Charles asked interestedly.

"Shirley fell with a jug of hot water," she responded now in tears. "Shit, how? How did it happen?"

"I don't really know, but I think she probably missed her step," she explained as she cried uncontrollably.

"Please be calm, can you hand over the phone to Tom," he requested as he held Margie's right hand to calm her down. "Okay," Dorcas accepted as she presented the phone to Tom. "Please talk with

Charles," she pleaded as she tried to wipe her tears with her right hand. Shirley cried harder in pains. "Sorry dear," Dorcas commiserated and knelt down in front of Tom.

"Hey man," Tom said strongly as he placed the phone on his ear. "Hey, what's up?"

"We want to rush her to the hospital, she is in serious pains," he replied. "Sorry dear," Dorcas chipped in as she blew some air on Shirley's hands through her mouth.

"Where is the most affected part?" Charles asked again. "Her hands," he answered as Shirley kept crying, "I want to take her to the general hospital," he added as he adjusted her on his laps.

"Alright, please do while I dress up and meet up with you." Charles said. "What's going on dear?" She asked as she stood erect but was signaled by Charles to keep calm. "Talk to me!" She shouted stubbornly.

"Ok. Baby please go and get my car key" Tom requested as he hung up the call. "Ok" she said sniffing and hastily rushed to the center table where Tom kept his brief case and collected the car key.

She returned in few seconds and gave it to him. "Thank you, please carry her" he instructed, Dorcas quickly stood up and opened her arms to carry her "Pull yourself together and stop crying" Tom said keenly and she agreed with disorganized nods

As he handed her over to Dorcas, Shirley abruptly increased her crying volume in pains "Sorry dear" Tom sympathized as he rushed to the door, opened it widely for Dorcas to pass through and locked the door behind him

They carefully entered the car and Tom drove off to the hospital.

"Babe, what happened?" Margie asked inquisitively, holding onto his singlet. "Can you calm down please,"

Charles pleaded holding her shoulder. "Ok," Margie agreed and took a deep breath. "I'm calm," she assured quietly.

"Shirley fell with a jug of hot water," Charles reported. "Oh God," Margie shouted and covered her mouth immediately. "Are they heading to the general hospital?" She inquired. "Yes," he replied and made a move to the bedroom. "I will quickly shower and go meet them," he asserted as he passed her, but she drew him back and pleaded that they should have breakfast and head to the hospital together.

"No, please go to work. You were absent yesterday. Moreover, you can come in the evening, please go," he pleaded intensely. "I insist please…ok, I will go to work from there," she assured as she pulled him to the dining.

"Okay," he said willingly, walked back to the dining and they sat down. "Please, we have to be fast," he cautioned.

"Alright," Margie said as she placed the pancakes on their plates with a picker.

CHAPTER FIFTHEEN

"I heard that"

After eating, they drove to Tokex General Hospital to see Shirley. On getting there, Margie rushed out of the car before Charles could pull out the car key from the ignition point.

"Easy dear," he advised as she pushed her hand into her hand bag's handle and slammed the car's door. Charles got down from the car and locked it entirely with its automatic remote. He walked fast to meet up with Margie who walked briskly towards the hospital's emergency section.

"I don't think she will be admitted in emergency," Charles suggested when he finally caught up with her. "Really, but she should be at emergency unit first, then transferred to the next section after seeing a doctor," she responded, shading her eyes from the rays of the sun with her right hand.

Charles turned to her with dimmed eyes, trying to accommodate the rays of the sun as well and questioned. "You think so?" And she nodded affirmatively. "I think I should put a call across to Tom," he added as he pushed his left hand into the left pocket of his trouser and brought out his phone. "OK," Margie said, still shading her eyes with her right hand.

As Charles connected Tom, instantly, Margie's phone rang.

"Hello, Steve," she greeted audibly. "Good morning, Margie. What's up, hope you are coming today?"

"I will come but a bit late," she answered, "I'm at the general hospital, my friend's daughter fell with a jug of hot water," she added immediately, stating her humble reasons to be late.

"Wow, I'm so sorry about that. How is she?" He commiserated. "We haven't seen her yet, but we will locate her soon," Margie answered as Charles signaled her to come over.

"Ok, please hasten up, we missed you yesterday. I guess you are still conscious of the boss's rage," Steve advised on the phone as Margie counted her steps towards Charles.

She shielded the phone's ear piece from the colliding breeze with her right hand to enable her hear him well. "Ok dear, I will be there in a jiffy."

"Alright, my regards to your friend's daughter, see you soon," he bided. "Thanks dear, see you soon," she replied as Steve hung up the call.

She hurriedly completed the remaining steps towards Charles and apologized for keeping him waiting. "I'm sorry, that was Steve," Charles harshly took a quick glance at her and replied, "You see; I would have preferred you come around in the evening."

"Come on, nothing will happen," she assured as she pulled him by the hand. "Honestly, I don't want stories from that ill-mannered boss of yours," he chipped in with concern, dragging his feet to slow down his moves as Margie laughed. "Relax, nothing will happen. I will quickly see her and head to the office," she asserted convincingly. "Hmmm, if you say so," he agreed willingly and freed up his legs to walk freely.

"So where are they?" Margie quickly asked as they approached the emergency unit's entrance. "Intensive care unit," he answered and continued without letting her reply. "I think we should ask of the place."

He quickly turned with surprise when Margie stopped walking with him and questioned curiously. "What?"

"Why the ICU?" she questioned back with her palms open. "I mean that should be just a burn and not like she is on life support," she added immediately with seriousness, raising her shoulder and brought down her right hand leaving the left one open.

"I don't know," Charles replied naively. "Come on let's go find them and stop being dramatic."

He quickly took a stop as he came by a male nurse that seemed approachable, making Margie to stop abruptly. "Good morning," Charles greeted and Margie waved with smiles. "Good morning," he replied, "Please, how do we locate ICU?" Charles inquired calmly. "The next building," he answered pointing at the building.

"Thank you," Charles said but got no reply. "I think he had a fight with his girlfriend this morning," Margie said. Charles giggled to that as they suddenly got a reply from the young man who they thought had walked away but unknowingly to them took the same direction with them.

"I heard that," he said meanly, staring at her with hate. "Sorry man," Charles stated apologetically as the male nurse walked away with no words and Margie mimicked his steps.

"Stop," Charles cautioned, drawing her back a bit as she stopped and sneered at him "You can be troublesome at times," Charles affirmed looking to identify the sign posts as they walked towards the building. "Really, that's why I'm unique," she responded sneering. "Yeah, I hope our son doesn't inherit that," Charles said with less concern.

Margie quickly hit his elbow angrily and he laughed and stated, "Come on babe, I was joking."

"I hate you," she said frowning. "I hate you too babe," Charles whispered to her left ear and they laughed.

They walked into the ICU and made their way to the receptionist's stand. They inquired for Shirley's ward and tried to locate it as directed.

Margie's place of work is characterized like that of a family, with so much cooperation, understanding, commitment and love amongst the staff. They always have each other's backs in times of trouble, both in the office and outside.

They never hesitate to make baseless excuses for each other's default or absence to their detriment. Molly always envied her for such a privilege to work in such institution and always wished to be favored like her.

Charles always fights against anything that will tarnish Margie's image at *Jewel drug store* where she works as a pharmacist because he knows what she benefits from working with them. He always defends the drug store no matter what, with the fear of not finding a better place if being sacked.

Despite the joy and serene environs witnessed in the store, they still lack a flexibly-mannered boss. Justin will always walk into the store and cease the good moments of his staff. He consciously ignores the welfare of his workers with his strong ambitions to be one of the best drug stores in Tokex.

He has all it takes to be the best. His academia, IQ, smartness, pharmaceutical experience and expertise are all on point. But he lacked the successful employer attributes he needs to pull through. Justin is capable of correcting his staff with a slap in the presence of a customer. His sensitivity for dirt can make him turn all his workers into cleansers to get rid of it.

In as much as he is engrossed with so must optimism for success and neglects for his staff, he still can identify his valuable staff which he

forgives their excesses willingly in order not to lose them.

With benefits of working together for so many years, they have learned and adapted to his bossy attitudes. They mapped out and mastered schemes to avoid his wrath. This has gone a long way to help them minimize his obvious harsh attitudes.

With time, they made *Jewel drug store*s appear as though it doesn't have arrogant manager but in few times, they lose their tactics and unleash his silly attitudes.

Margie didn't worry about him as they searched for Shirley, for she knows how to handle him. As they walked from one ward and passage into another, they kept encountering jams on critically ill patients.

These sights not only made her pity their situations but also disgust her. "This is why I hate hospitals," she complained with scowls as they broke free of a man wheeled to his room with bandages all over his body, revealing only his mouth, nose and eyes.

"Sorry dear," Charles sympathized. "Yeah, now I remember. I had that early morning sickness again today," she chipped in, stealing glances on him as they walked side by side. "Really," Charles retorted with surprise. "Yes, I had fever, body pains, cold and I vomited too. But it all calmed down as I began do morning chores," she explained as she demonstrated the level of pain she had.

"I suggest you see a doctor," Charles advised meekly. "I will," she accepted as she caught sight of the children's ward boldly written on its entrance. "Finally, we found the damn ward," she asserted with relief. "Yeah, now we have to locate room seventeen," Charles said as they walked into the ward and kept looking up to the top of each room's door, to ascertain which one matches with the one they are searching for.

Charles saw the room number first and called Margie's attention to it. "This is it"

Margie knocked on the door, as Charles impatiently opened it. They strode into the room, only to meet the presence of the doctor in charge of Shirley's condition standing with Tom and Dorcas.

"Good morning, doctor," Charles and Margie greeted after another. "Good morning," he relied with glares of confusion. "Are we safe?" He asked interestedly, and then Tom quickly intervened. "Yes, this is my friend and his wife."

"Okay," he answered and turned to the medical report book he was filling before they walked in.

"How is she?" Margie asked passionately.

"She is better now," Dorcas replied in a low tone.

Shirley is fast asleep; she was injected with a pain relief drug to enable her battle less with her pain. On her left and right are huge bolsters that controlled her body movements while sleeping, to prevent her from bursting the inflammations she has on her skin. By her right, close to the mini table the doctor bent on, is an infusion stand, on which an intravenous fluid is being injected into her to compensate for the fluid needed to accommodate fluid loss due to inflammation

She lay uprightly on the bed, wearing pants. As soon as they got to the hospital, her clothes were stripped off to avoid worsening the present situation. In few minutes, the affected parts became soft and swollen, filled with water. The epidermal layer became light and fragile such that a little touch can rupture the swollen sacs.

The doctor swiftly turned to them and they turned anxiously to him as well to hear what he has to say.

"Uhmm," he muttered and slipped his right hand into his trousers' pocket. "Unfortunately, Shirley is caught up in this condition, but not to worry, it is not beyond our capability," he assured, throwing glances at them individually as they nodded in agreement.

He pulled out his hand from his pocket to enable him illustrate better and continued, "Shirley is affected with what we call, second degree burn. This occurs when the epidermis or uppermost layer of the skin and the dermis are affected. Other structures such as the sweat glands, hair follicles and so on can also be affected," he paused and glanced at them to ensure they understood him and continued when they nodded.

"Its symptoms include: blisters, pains, swollen epidermal layer also known as edema, decreased blood flow and so on."

He paced forward, close to her bed to point at her and ease

their understanding towards what he is about to tell them.

"Based on our classification for burns, she has moderate burns, involving just 13% BSA. BSA means Burned Surface Area. Also, involvement of the hands, feet and face; so, any patient with these features are obliged to be admitted in the hospital," he elucidated further as they kept listening calmly.

"As we can see, Shirley has these features, but do not panic for if you cooperate with the medical team in charge, she will be out of here in two weeks. So unfortunately, you ignorantly did not pull off her clothes immediately this happened, for if you had done that, the severity wouldn't have been this much, but relax, it's not yet bad," he detailed as Dorcas breathed out heavily.

"So, that is it. The rest of the team will be here shortly, I mean a nurse, pharmacist and a dietitian and probably a dermatologist, if needed," he said as he prepared to leave.

"But there was a nurse who admitted us, is she the one we are to expect?" Tom asked curiously.

"I guess, that must be an emergency nurse whose shift will soon be over. You will get a new one," he answered with smiles.

"Any problem? You don't like her services?" The doctor questioned keenly. "Not at all, just wanted to know," Tom said.

"Alright, I will leave you all right now. All you need to do is to cooperate with us and she will be strong again in no time," the doctor advised. "Ok, thank you."

"Honestly, I never expected this," Dorcas lamented, staring at her helpless daughter. "Don't blame yourself for this, Dorcas," Margie advised and held her hand. "Thank you," she replied inaudibly. "Shouldn't you be at work?"

Dorcas asked, "Yeah, but…" Margie replied but was interrupted.

"But what? You were absent yesterday," Tom chipped in. "Yes," she answered "I wanted to see her first," she added before Tom could utter a word

"Please go to work, as you can see she is fine," Dorcas said, pointing at Shirley, she slowly stepped closer to Margie, held her right elbow and continued.

"I informed Ginika that you will be coming. So, you will have to go and see her without me, I already explained certain things to her. Please go" Dorcas pleaded. Margie couldn't hold back her feelings of gratitude as she smiled to Dorcas's kind gestures. She swiftly held her hands together uprightly to her chest and appreciated her with smiles.

"Oh my God that's so nice of you, Thank you so much."

"Alright, off I go. Take good care of yourselves and Shirley. I will be back soon," she uttered as she turned to her husband.

"Ok, we will. Thanks for coming," Tom appreciated with smiles. "Yeah, babe, I have to run. Take good care of yourself," she bided as he pecked her forehead. "I will and you too," he replied and they hugged each other.

The Chopkins residence appears so desolate unlike before, the abode's composure diminished drastically sequel to Robin's death and Molly's arrest. They made up the dwelling's sparks of liveliness especially in the morning and odd hours.

With the situation at hand one could comfortably search for them at the most insignificant site to ascertain what has gone wrong. Regrettably, they are far beyond reach.

The television portrayed an early morning section of encounter with God. With its volume at its peak, the young pastor handling the preaching lauded his voice to every edge of the deserted dwelling.

The communication media has this norm of carrying out its activities cautiously without minding if anybody is listening. They always believe the fact that, so long as their frequency goes, so do people tune in and out of it. At the Chopkin's residence, the device was carefully tuned in, with no audience.

Perhaps, the volume is outrageously thunderous, but beheld no ears to deafen with its effects. The sofas became dusty in few days. Although, they seem not to be, but a single bit of the tip of a finger can leave a mark of difference on that part. The side chairs miss its users; the center table lost its value.

Generally, every property in the house exhibits gloominess to Robin and Molly's absence. Although, they filed no complaint with regards to their idealness, one can easily detect that something is wrong somewhere.

Less activity in the kitchen does not make any significant difference to other's static state, all remains the same.

Without prior notice, every sphere of Robin's room displays a clear existence of masculinity. His personal belongings miss his presence such that every surface can be marked with the dusty suspensions on them. Not knowing he had already passed away, they wait for his return.

Molly's companions all stood motionless waiting to welcome her any day she returns. Her room radiates an absolute tranquility, which signifies that the only one, who makes it lively by all means, isn't available. In her absence they exhibit a recognizable state of inability to communicate verbally, to confirm that they are non-living creatures.

Each keeps moping at the particular direction it is facing. She gave them the sense of belonging and attributed them with qualities they do not have naturally. The last time they had contact was before Robin's death which has indirectly limited their access to her for some time.

Susan never minded her desolated home rather kicked off with her normal daily activities sooner than expected. As the clock kept ticking so did her rage became inevitable. Each passing second keeps reaffirming her determination to deal with everyone involved in Robin's death, directly or indirectly.

She dressed up tightly, on an ash colored suit and trouser, a white inner long-sleeved shirt and a red tie. She flawlessly applied her makeup, fitted in her hair into her wig and tucked in the white shirt. She breathed out heavily and tilted up her feet a bit to be able to reach out to her red tie, handing directly above her standing mirror.

She placed back the sole of her foots on its original positions, bearing the tie on her right hand. She positioned the left edge of the tie on her left hand and pulled it with her right hand to the other edge, to achieve an accurate length that can make a tie round her neck.

Susan gently crossed the tie over her head and raised her collar to fit it in. Just then she heard an ambulance's horn, she quickly rushed to the window to get a clear view of the convoy conveying the corpse. When she looked closely, she caught a quick glance of a dismayed young woman, who sat feebly in front of a car following the ambulance.

Unfortunately, she couldn't capture her face due to the tinted glasses she was wearing. A whole lot rushed through her mind with this sight. Ruthlessly, she closed the curtain, rushed and grabbed her hand bag on the table, waggled her hands vigorously in it and brought out her phone.

She quickly dialed the police station's number. When she placed the phone on her ear, she slotted in two of her right finger into her trousers' belt holder, making her thumb to lap on her waist. She kept turning towards the window as she breathed fast, waiting for the officers to pick up.

Surprisingly, she was instructed to leave a voicemail for the police station as no one could pick up. "What!" She acclaimed with astonishment on hearing that. "What's going on? Does it mean no one is on duty?"She questioned herself in a low-tone

She decided to call again to clear her intense doubts. This time, an officer picked up the call and said.

"Good morning, this is Officer Joe, how can I help you?"

She sharply looked up to the ceiling with so much joy and relief, she answered, "Uhmm,

I'm Susan Chopkins, I want to inquire if Molly Chopkins is still in your custody?"

"You mean your daughter?" Officer Joe asked inquisitively to ascertain her request.

"Yes, Molly Chopkins," she replied briskly as she held her lower lip with her incisors, anticipating for his answer

"Yes she is," he replied almost immediately.

"Please can you check to verify this?" She requested and got no reply.

She guessed he went to check if she is still available and her tension got to its height. To and fro the length of the bed she paced curiously until she heard his voice, and stood still instantaneously.

"She is still in our custody," the police officer affirmed.

She sighed with a drooped face of relief and collapsed into the bed backwardly. "Alright, thanks," she succinctly replied to the officer's surprise, who expected more demands. "Ok, take care," he hung up the call.

Susan sluggishly placed the phone on her stomach, with her hands joined together above it. She briefly bothered about the lady she just saw in front of the ambulance that passed by few minutes ago.

Still wondering who could resemble Molly that much, she calmly turned to the window by which she stood and gazed at it for some seconds as the air from outside puffed its silky curtain swiftly into the room.

She quickly sits up on the bed and looks around in a confused manner as she is almost certain of what she saw. In no time she quickly waved it off her mind, holding onto the assurance the officer gave her.

She stands up energetically and walked to her dressing table. Kept her phone on the table and sat down on the already pulled out chair, she selected her favorite jewelries from their collections and wore them. Her beauty became

solidified with those accessories, as she placed the watch on her wrist; she caught a glance of herself on the mirror and took her time to admonish herself.

Although, she looks alright, she still feels herself dangling in an empty room. She slowly pushed her hair backwards and took a deep breath to overshadow her emotions.

Suddenly her phone rings, she hastily picked it when she saw the caller is Vanessa, "Hello," she said as she placed the phone on her ear.

"Good morning, Ma."

"Good morning, I have been expecting your call, how is it going?" Susan questioned curiously. She quickly stood up and walked to her shoe rack. She made a choice of the one she wants and walked back to her former position with it, as Vanessa kept on explaining things to her on phone.

"Fine, I understand. His burial date has been fixed, I will text it to you shortly," Susan retorted as she slots her left leg into the shoe.

"Alright, take care dear," she hung up.

Her mood brightened after the call with Vanessa; she quickly took her phone and handbag and drove out.

When Margie entered the drug store, she hastily greeted everyone in sight and headed to her office.

"Good to have you back," Steve declared joyfully on seeing her as Margie smiled back happily. They hugged each other friendly, as they left each other's warmth; Margie quickly reminded, "I have to go sort myself out with Justin"

"Yeah, please run," Steve said supportively as Margie rushed out.

Justin is busy on his desk with his eyes fixed on his laptop, his mean gaze on the screen shows something is wrong somewhere. He sluggishly removed the site, with the notion that it's not his business. He drew his seat closer, clicked on Google search engine and typed *Cipratizaxole*. When he opened one of the journals listed, he quickly pounced into it to squeeze out information the journal has on it.

As he kept on reading, he heard a knock on the door and granted permission for entry. Margie slowly entered with a dull face, stood by his shelf and greeted.

"Good morning."

"Good morning," he answered raising his eyes and forehead. "Welcome," he added and fixed back his gaze on the laptop.

"How is your friend coping with the scandal?" He asked before Margie could say anything.

"She is doing well," Margie answered.

"You know; I think she should channel her cloning research to crisis such as the recent chaos at the limestone site and not on ending a precious life," he asserted speedily to Margie's surprise.

"Chaos at the limestone site?" She hurriedly asked with squinted eyes of curiosity.

"Yes, it's everywhere, the residents of Maryland district have been ordered to leave the premises to avoid being victims of the crisis," he explained further. Just then, Margie remembered she missed the Morning's news. "Wow," she acclaimed.

"You haven't heard about it?"

"Yes," she replied innocently.

"Come and see," he requested as Margie gently came forward, he quickly minimized what he was reading and went back to the site he had been looking at. He turned the laptop to Margie's direction for her to confirm it.

"Wow, this is serious," she commented sadly as she slowly sat down on the client's seat. "For how long has this been happening?" She inquired.

"It started early this morning. The news said Gozax army struck first, based on an order from the government to take the site back."

"Wow, I thought this has been settled, why take us back to havoc again?" Margie asked again with dismay.

"I don't know. But, I think Molly's research should be put into use now," he advised and turned his laptop to himself.

"Hmm," Margie breathed out heavily. "God help us," she added and paused for a while and continued.

"Sir,"

"Yes," he answered and looked up to her.

"Please I will like to seek for your permission to extend my lunch time to an hour," she requested meekly and hurriedly went further to explain as she noticed the change on his face.

"I need to secure a lawyer for Molly. On my way, I got a call from her mother's lawyer that a case has been filled against her, please sir."

"Why will she call you?" Justin questioned nosily.

"I am Molly's next of kin for now," she carefully answered.

"I see," he asserted with raised eyebrows as he tossed his pen around on his desk.

After few seconds of silence and considerations, he permitted her without much queries.

"Thank you, sir," she thanked him cheerfully and stood up to leave.

"Ask Steve to cover up for the one hour," he ordered.

"I will," she replied and left.

His smooth reactions perplexed her; she wondered if he is the one she just discussed with. She rushed back to her office jubilantly to share her experience with Steve.

As they kept chatting, her phone rang.

"It's Charles," she excused herself and picked the call. "Hi dear,"

"Hey babe, how are you?"

"I'm fine, and you?"

"I'm fine, please be careful, the limestone site is under attack. Do not hesitate to leave any environment that eventually becomes harmful please," he requested keenly.

"Ok, I will be safe. Stay safe too," she advised.

"Ok, bye," he bided and hung up.

CHAPTER SIXTHEEN

Scale of innocence

Margie got to *Absolute Justice Firm* on an appointment with Ginika. Although, she accepted to hire Ginika based on persuasions from her husband and Dorcas, she still inwardly had doubts about her capabilities but has no option than to settle for her services.

Margie displayed a hasty manner in her activities at the firm to enable her bit the limited time she has. She packed her car on one of the vacant spaces at the parking lot and briskly walked into the building.

She intentionally strode to the receptionist with smiles, to alleviate the past encounter they had on her previous visit. She quickly removed her handbag from her shoulder, placed it on the receptionist desk and said with smiles before the receptionist could say anything

"Good morning, please I'm here to see Ginika Emechelu."

She kept shifting her legs restlessly to show she is in haste. Unfortunately, the receptionist had series of questions to ask despite the familiarity.

"Do you have an appointment with her?" The receptionist questioned and opened her computer to view the shortlisted appointments.

"Yes, I do," Margie answered and breathed out impatiently.

"I can see an appointment scheduled for this same time but by Dr. Dorcas Smith…" the receptionist said but was quickly interrupted by Margie.

"Yes, she referred me to her,"

"Ok, please I will have to confirm that," the receptionist asserted and hastily picked the company's intercommunication device to place a call to Ginika.

Suddenly, the cheerful smiles Margie had disappeared as she rested her elbows on the receptionist desk, tapped her forehead with her right palm and muttered inaudibly, while the receptionist spoke with Ginika on phone.

"I don't have time for this."

In few seconds, the receptionist got the confirmation and approval she needed. Then, she looked up to Margie whose cheerful mood already fluctuated into a stressed mood and directed her calmly to avoid increasing her bad mood.

"Please, take the elevator to the fifth floor, and then the seventh office by your left is her office."

"Thank You," Margie said and hurriedly carried her bag.

At the front of the elevator stood a huge looking young man. He dressed in a fitted doorman's uniform and has a contraband checking device on his left hand with which he uses to determine if any visitor to the firm has any harmful object in their possession.

At the sight of the young man, Margie comprehended another obstacle to overcome. Despite her impatient state she didn't want to create any illogical scene.

When she got to the doorman, he signaled her to stop with his right hand and tried to place the gadget on her but she queried him immediately.

"Please I have been searched over there," she said pointing at the main entrance. "Why this? That's the security protocol," he replied sternly.

"Interesting, so the mean look is also part of the security protocol?" Margie smartly asked.

"Please let me do my job."

She coolly raised her hands to her shoulder level to conserve the little time she has, he touched her thighs, waist, rib cages, chest, and handbag with the gadget. The gadget signaled a green color showing

she is free of any harmful object.

The doorman pressed the open button of the elevator's door and it opened. Surprisingly, she noticed when she entered, that an unknown device still scanned her before the door closed and she regrettably uttered to the doorman's hearing.

"Absolutely, your security system sucks."

Immediately, the doorman turned sharply as he didn't hear her well and asked, "What?" But was deliberately ignored.

She knocked on Ginika's door and got a response to enter. Ginika observed her expression and inquired for the reason.

"You look saddened? What's the problem?" She asked.

"Yes, your security system is pathetic," Margie replied aggressively as she placed her handbag on her laps.

"Wow, I'm sorry but that's the protocol and they are helplessly doing their job," she carefully explained as Margie quickly drew forward to clearly state her reasons.

"Personally, I think its tiring, such that one in a hurry can be choked of time," Margie deplorably retorted.

"Now, it has to do with time factor," she asserted and placed her hands on her desk. "A client with a relaxed mind will not look into all that except in cases of impatient temperament."

Margie felt mined of all the reasons she could give to back up her complaint but still stressed on redress.

"I still think it's not encouraging and something should be done about it because with this kind of experience one can easily loose interest of coming here."

"Ok, that will be looked into," Ginika humbly replied smiling and continued, "Good morning by the way."

"Good morning dear, sorry for stressing you with my worries," Margie apologetically replied with smiles too.

"That's not a problem at all," she said as Margie nodded in reply.

Ginika gently pushed her laptop to her right hand side to enable her see Margie's face. She carefully minimized what she was working on to create less distractions and placed her fingers on the desk in a joint manner.

"So, Dorcas explained everything involved in Molly's case to me but I still want to converse with you," Ginika said and paused to ensure Margie understood her. Margie affirmatively nodded to what she said and she continued.

"First, why did you choose me?"

"Because Dorcas highly recommended you and there is

no other option, since other good lawyers I know went for the supposed conference," Margie briefly explained.

She picked up her pen on the desk slowly and curiously asked to Margie's surprise.

"Alright, do you think Molly is innocent?"

Margie took her time to stare at Ginika for some seconds and answered strongly with certainty, "Yes, she is."

"Ok, please relax, there is no cause for alarm," Ginika cautioned calmly.

"Why do you ask?" She irascibly asked with incredible eyes of curiosity.

"Unfortunately, Molly might be guilty," she said in a low tone as Margie regressed back on the seat she sat on sadly.

"By this I mean that the probability of proving her innocent is very low, based on the fact that there is no prior consent of the mother, the skillful lawyer Susan hired and

suspicious attitudes and utterances that might have been captured by the camera, which I am sure Vanessa won't ignore," she carefully detailed.

With this fact Ginika just revealed, Margie felt weakened to her bones because she knew all Ginika pointed out is true.

She weakly closed her eyes for some seconds to think of the logical chances left, breathed out heavily and asked almost hopelessly in a low tone."So, there is no hope?"

"Of course, there is hope. That's why there is the court, chief judge, witnesses, constitution, logical defenses and me to help defend her the way we can in our various ways," she said vehemently with smiles and leaned back on her seat.

"Hmmm, I'm scared," Margie expressed with an unhappy face.

"Relax, it's part of my duty to reveal to my clients the

chances of winning any case no matter how easy the case and how innocent my client may be," She carefully explained to reduce Margie's fear.

Margie quickly sat up on her sit, rested her hands on the desk and looked her in the eyeballs. Her emotions overshadowed her reasoning such that all she could think of is how Molly will survive the prison's harsh environment and activities for the rest of her life. Her eye socket got drenched with tears immediately, as her voice began shaking vulnerably and almost inaudible.

"Please, do all it takes, I might not prove this but I know Molly is innocent. Robin's death was the least outcome she envisaged for that cloning trial. Please help her with all you can do please. We are hoping on you, please."

"It's ok my dear, all hope is not lost, I will do my best and I assure you Molly will be out of

jail in no time. Please be encouraged, I will schedule a visit time with her and have a heart to heart talk with her tomorrow. I will do my best," Ginika toughly assured.

"Ok, thank you so much," she replied feeling a bit goaded and continued as she noticed she is running out of time.

"Please what is your service charge? I'm running out of time."

"Ok. About that, I charge one thousand dollars per court appearance," she answered amicably.

"Ok, that's fair. We are good to go," Margie smiled in acceptance.

"Alright, you…" she muttered as she turned to her left and tried to pull out a fresh client's folder from her shelf.

She opened the folder and placed it in front of Margie, the folder contains the statement of agreement document, client's details form, court proceedings report and payment chart based on each court appearance. "You will have to sign here," she added pointing to where Margie has to sign as next of kin.

She handed over her pen to her and she carefully appended her signature. As Ginika turned the folder to herself, she said,

"Thank you, I will surely keep in touch and notify you when a date for court hearing is fixed. Also, I will sign in as her lawyer after visiting her tomorrow and notify the court that we are aware that the case has being filed."

"Ok, thank you very much, please I will have to run," Margie stated and pulled up her hand bag's handle, preparing to leave.

Once more, Ginika quickly turned the document to her.

"One more thing please, your phone number and residential address," she requested pointing at the vacant space for it.

"Ok," she replied, collected her pen again and wrote down all she requested for

"Thank you, that's all. I guess we see when next it is necessary," she stated with smiles as Margie speedily stood up.

"Alright," she said affirmatively.

They shook hands with each other, bided goodbye and Margie hurriedly rushed out in order to meet up with the little time she has left.

Susan stepped into her former work place with so much energy emanating from her steps, attire, body gestures and smiles.

Her former coworkers were startled on seeing her. Some quickly thought she has being called back to work while some dim minded ones hastily wondered if she should be mourning her only son's demise or showing off surprise visits.

"Hey," she said and waved at the doorman. He replied almost immediately sluggishly mumbling his word. "Hey"

Susan quickly noticed he couldn't recognize her and pulled out the tinted eye glass she is wearing. Her bold smiles still seemed awkward to him as his face displayed wrinkles of uncertainty because he couldn't recognize her.

"I'm Susan," she declared smiling and extending her right hand for a hand shake.

"Henry," he retorted as they shook hands. "It's my pleasure to meet you, welcome to *Miles Publications,*" he added gracefully in an official manner.

"Thank you," she appreciated as they let go of their hands. "I guess you are new here," she added and he nodded affirmatively.

"Can I help you in any way?" He asked curiously.

"Not at all, I used to work here…" she answered as Prisca suddenly walked up to them.

With so much surprise, she curiously asked with opened palms, "Susan, why are you here?"

"You are supposed to be at home resting" Prisca added without letting Susan say a word.

"I think I'm getting home sick by the day, I need to stretch out. How are you?" Susan answered.

"I am fine, but don't you think…" Prisca said as Susan interrupted her immediately. "Give me a break Prisca, I am fine too."

"Ok, if you say so."

"How has work been?" Susan inquired as they turned towards the reception.

"Work has been…" Prisca answered and suddenly went indistinct vocally as Susan turned back to the doorman and said, "It's nice speaking to you Henry."

"Same here enjoy your day," he said and turned back to his duty.

Susan waved to the receptionists and mounted the stairs with Prisca. As they climbed, they discussed of the Xylom limestone's crisis as they climbed each stair after another.

"I think Gozax needs a break on crisis, we have had more than enough in the past two decades. Not like there is any improvement on getting it back. The situation gets worse by the day," Prisca lamented and stopped momentarily, facing Susan to buttress her point.

"Residents of Maryland district are displaced all over the country, looking for refuge. Eric and Nikelite constructions had to hire a residential building at Leach district to accommodate their displaced workers for the time being," Prisca further explained.

"Really!"

"Yes, this entire charade is uncalled for. Work hasn't been easy since two days ago, not to talk of losses pertaining to this crisis."

"Wow, so sorry. I think Miles and Nikelite workers are lucky enough to have bosses that look out for them in times like this," Susan briefly added stylishly and passed Prisca by, heading up the stairs.

As Prisca couldn't comprehend her nonchalant response, she quickly turned and acclaimed meanly in a high tune. "Excuse me!"

"What?" Susan shouted back with a backup smile and stopped. "Come on, what will you have me say? I mean, the government is on the right track, same as their opponent. Whoever that is affected should hid to their warnings and leave that vicinity," she added meanly and turned, but was stopped again by Prisca's opinion.

"Without considering how they will cope with it?"

"Prisca you worry too much, there is always a way out, like the NGOs, family, friends and bosses like Eric and Nikelite. See…" she responded defensively raising her shoulders.

"I can't believe you right now," Prisca said and walked up. "Really Prisca, but you know I just said the truth," she said as Prisca sharply turned to her and retorted spitefully,

"The truth? You speak like you haven't lost enough to this fight!"

Prisca's last statement shocked Susan; her nursed pains became bruised again. Suddenly, she lost all efforts of argument she had. Then, she calmly walked up to the next stair to which Prisca stood and warned angrily.

"Don't go down that lane with me."

"I'm sorry," Prisca apologetically, but was ignored.

"Hey, I'm sorry," Prisca said again making Susan to pause. She could have walked up to her destination but was stopped again by the disguised voice of friendship Molly, Robin, Margie and every other reasonable person feared. She reluctantly turned to her and said to reinforce what they share.

"It's okay. Please watch it next time."

"Thank you," she replied and increased her pace to meet up with her.

"I guess you came for Eric?" She added smiling boldly as they walk side by side.

"Yes," Susan replied cheerfully.

"That's cool," she responded with mischievous smiles that depicted suppressed rage.

"Less I forget," she said as Prisca quickly casted her keen

gaze into Susan's eyes. "Ok, I'm all ears," she replied and they stopped remotely.

CHAPTER SEVENTEEN

The most unforeseen news

Susan appears still for few seconds that seems like hours, Prisca repeatedly changes her body positions to suit her inquisitive steers, her right sleeve jerks gently, concurrently to the gentle breeze from a standing air conditioner by her right as she waits patiently for Susan to speak up.

Susan's static state isn't orchestrated by Prisca's intolerable gawks but the burden of the news she bears. Her tightened grip to her hand bag loosened up as her eye lashes shakes enabling her eyes to blink uncontrollably.

As she involuntarily exhibited her discomfort, countless unimaginable thoughts plummeted into Prisca's mind like dew drops. She curiously boosted each of these drops of thought in deep search for the right reasons to suit Susan's disquiet. Her snooping mind swerved through a whole lot in such a limited time; unfortunately she couldn't point a finger to what it could be.

Just then, Susan pretentiously looks speedily at her wrist probably to ascertain the time but the glance was too quick to conclude she did. Instantaneously, her fairly wet gloomy eyes fell back on Prisca's face. Prisca's current facial expression passed on a weird but quick message to her "I'm waiting…"At that moment, she realized the time duration she has taken to mutter her heavy words.

Prisca's nosey mind bumped into a drop of thought that made her scowl unnoticeably. "Could she be pregnant for Eric?" Her neck vein became visible spontaneously such that Susan could notice, prompting her to speak out forcefully.

"Robin's burial date has been fixed," she managed to say and clamped her painted lips inwardly.

"What?" Prisca reacted thriftily to the news she least expected. "That's too sudden…" she added with a disenchanted-squeezed face without allowing a word from Susan and continued. "It's barely a week and…"

"I know…" Susan succinctly interrupted with grief. "Prisca, his demise was the last thing I saw coming, its draining me," she smoldered meanly. "I can't even sleep…the nightmares, the memories, his glimpses… are still fresh and it pierces my heart painfully."

"Prisca, he was my only son… I might seem so strong and happy but deep down… I am brutally wounded. Even at this time, I still can't imagine he is dead… Molly brought the worse to me Prisca." She excessively lamented, closed her eyes and tilted her neck to her right shoulder to absorb her grief and pain. Her sorrow touched Prisca's heart warmly, despite her confused state; she still managed to maintain her stand.

"But, that doesn't mean he should be laid to rest so soon, it's not up to a week of his death Susan, what will people say?"

Unfortunately, Susan already dealt with Prisca's question long before Robin's death, her sudden welcoming smiles appeared like a mockery to Prisca –*What will people say?* - Susan repeated reluctantly.

People's opinion became irrelevant few months after Donald's death; they thought, said and gossiped all sorts of things about Susan. She always cried on hearing any of the lies. The more she cried, the more the untruth penetrated, she tried to prove them wrong rather it seemed she cheered them up. With time, she discovered she had no right to what people's choice of thought, belief and perspective.

On a very good morning she bumped into a life striking leaflet on Donald's shelf which said, "You tell people the truth, they believe what they want…"

She repeatedly ruminated through these words until it sunk deep into her mind. It configured her mindset, thoughts and feelings into a tough one. Immediately, she assumed her survival scheme of not listening to what people have to say. So, for Robin's case, her mind is already made up.

"I don't care," she carelessly replied and to the door in front of her.

Prisca's gloomy face depicted she isn't abreast with her decision and secondly, Susan headed for the most inappropriate office. "What of Molly, is she coming?" she quickly asked almost inaudibly as she turned, making Susan to stop immediately in front of the door as if she felt a sharp itch, then she turned calmly and said to Prisca's surprise.

"She is not…"

"Why?" She hastily asked.

"I'm behind schedule, I'll call you later," she replied emotionlessly and opened the door.

When the door finally closed on her face, Prisca's rage and anger became real and fierce such that the subsequent activity for the day became muddled. Her jealousy for Susan's closeness to Eric solidified its roots by the day.

The bus Margie boarded back to her place of work seems comforting and notable. She took few steps into the nearest vacant seat and gently sat down, her hang bag had quickly launched itself on the seat before her making her sit directly on it, maybe it was tired of the day's stress too.

The human muscles has a natural way of showing how stressed out an individual is, even though Margie has been

agile with her activities for the day but the moment she took a seat in the bus the energetic spirit that guided her footsteps became hazy.

She lazily forced out her bag with strained facial expression each time she tried to pull it out. Just then, in relief, she voluntarily pulled in her chicks gently to puff out some hot air from her mouth. Instantaneously, she heard an apologetic voice say, "I'm sorry please." She didn't bother to look onto the face to see who it is but gently squeezed her toes in pain as she shifted her feet inside her sitting space. The unfamiliar face had stamped on her toes.

As she slacked into her seat and held her hand bag to her chest, she began to observe the fresh and unlikely features the bus contained. "New Transport Company," she reflected and shook it off her mind at that moment.

Each stop the bus made irritated her to her marrows

and made her harbor regrets on why her car would develop fault on this busy day of hers. As she wished the bus will move wait less at every bus stop and move faster, she also longed for more time to relax more.

Her mixed feeling quickly exuded her as her phone began to vibrate. She responded to the stimuli by quickly slotting her hand into her hand bag to bring out her phone. At the time she managed to bring it out, she had already missed the call from Dorcas. Clearly, she thought Dorcas will be calling her to find out about her meeting with Ginika.

She gently placed her right thumb on the center of the phone and dragged the dial sign to the right side. In her relaxed state she quietly placed the phone's speaker on her right ear in order to hear her.

"Hey Margie," Dorcas greeted.

"Hey, how is Shirley?"

"She is awake now," Dorcas replied confidently. "How did it go with Ginika?"

"Oh that," she muttered and breathed out heavily. "It went well, she said she will indicate as Molly's lawyer and show consent to the lawsuit."

"Alright, nice one. One more thing," Dorcas replied immediately.

"Ok?" Margie sluggishly muttered again in anticipation to what Dorcas wants to tell her.

"I believe Molly will be out of jail in no time," Dorcas commiserated sanguinely as Margie gently caressed her forehead in relief making her eyes to go dim slightly. In a sluggish manner she wrapped her right hand around the glass cup with an orange-colored liquid in it which stood before her and made her way to the sitting room where Charles sat to grab the city's happenings on television.

"Alright, I appreciate," she replied calmly and took a sip from the glass of orange juice entrusted in her right hand. All Charles could comprehend as she approached was goodbye chatters she is having with her caller.

As Margie swiftly collapsed into the cushion next to him, he opened up his curious mind to her. "Who's that?"

"Oh, that was Molly," she lied pretentiously with a raised eyebrow in eagerness of Charles' response. Unsurprisingly, Charles quickly sat up and asked with a tight curious gaze on his wife, "Molly? How?"

After a while, Margie bursts into laugher. "It was Dorcas."

"What's new?" She asked with a quick glance at the television implying that she needed an update about the news. Charles quietly patted on the cushion trying to remember all he has gotten from the evening news.

"Well…" he uttered as he fleetly moved his lips to the left. Margie softly dropped her phone and the glass of juice on the side stool by her left. "Nothing much…"

"The limestone crisis is still on and is getting worse," he muttered sympathetically as Margie conjoined with a deplorable face. "Secondly; the national economy is becoming an itch to the government," he added as Margie worriedly replied, "Why?"

"The President concluded his speech just before you came in. He lamented so much on the rival implication of this new business trend, uhm-mm, digital currency which comprises of Bitcoin, Lois coin, and the latest called Alien coin," he explained diligently. "How is that an economic itch?" Margie speedily interrupted as she couldn't grasp the fact he stated.

"Easy…" he advised with smiles and adjusted on his seat

to make it clearer, "This is, from his speech, he stated that the minister of finance has carefully examined the implications of this business and discovered that the rate of financial liquidity because of online trading with these digital currencies has increased by 85%, owning to the fact that almost every living being in the country has traded for digital currencies with their entire savings leading to a drastic decrease in cash flow and as such can lead to inflation."

"They should print new notes then if cash flow is now an excuse," She sloppily replied. "It doesn't work like that my darling; this percentage of liquidity is pertained just to the masses not to talk of the government's percentage. He also mention of a ban on digital currency but declared that after several deliberations that it isn't the safest option but pleaded with the people to think of their future and trade

wisely," he explained further as Margie listened keenly.

"Obviously, people won't listen to that else he devises another…" She replied as Charles quickly interrupted. "He mentioned of venturing into any scheme that will enhance the nation's fight for the limestone."

"A scheme? Coupled with the crisis and economic slope?" she sharply asked as she seated up to make her way to the room. "He is not serious," she sketchily added while Charles tried to put up laughter.

"Again, sorry darling," he hurriedly interrupted her with a shocking question as she tried to stand up. "Did you hear anything about Robin?"

In amazement, she replied, "Robin? You mean Robin Chopkins? Any problem?" she asked curiously but got an answer that got to her marrows. "While in the office, I heard that his funeral is tomorrow. Eric mistakenly told Tom over a discussion on phone. He never thought Tom would be concerned about it; it's in three days time. Did you…"

"What!" Margie angrily interrupted as she promptly sprang up from the cushion on which she sat as her phone instantly rang out peacefully. "Please calm down, I thought you knew about it," Charles worrisomely advised in an attempt to slake her rage as Margie quickly turned to her phone.

"It's Ginika," she replied with a quick peek at him. "Hello," she answered as she placed the phone on her left ear.

"Hello," Ginika replied "Margie I'm so sorry I am calling you this late. I will be with Molly tomorrow for a heart to heart discussion and I will love for you to be there. Lastly and unfortunately…"

"Are you aware that Robin will be laid to rest tomorrow?" She asked meanly as she paced about. "Yes, I did everything I cou…" Ginika tried to answer

but was shunned again. "For Christ's sake, you are Molly's lawyer, and should act as such. She deserves to pay her only blood brother this last respect," Margie helplessly stated.

"I am fully sentient to all that, and trust me I did all within my power to…"

Ginika explained as Margie consciously muttered "Jesus Christ!" in pains, her left hand with which she held the phone drifted down and she sank into the cushion again. Whispers of Ginika's voice can still be heard on the phone but Margie's hopelessness could not let her hear her out.

After few seconds of pondering on a remedy, without getting any, she gave in and lethargically placed her phone back on her ear. "Trust me, I will fix this. I am putting in all my efforts into this and we will be victorious," Ginika incited. "Alright, thank you. I will see you tomorrow," Margie peacefully said in soreness and ended the call.

For the first time, she ran out of aid for Molly. Her helplessness drenched her thoughts in a way that it couldn't think straight momentarily. All that came to her mind is "Poor Molly, Poor Molly."

Charles hurriedly sat beside her, cuddling her by the shoulder in consolation as he whispered, "All will be well my love."

CHAPTER EIGHTEEN

Indeed, death isn't an excuse

If there would be anyone to usher the police officers into their offices the next morning, it would be Margie. As the officers obliviously walked into their offices, she sat patiently at the reception in order to see Molly. She kept on waiting to the tick tocks of the wall clock that hung on the wall directly opposite her, on the strike of 8am; she hurriedly stood up and moved towards the counter.

The police officer who was on night shift had already informed the incumbent of the aim of Margie's early arrival. As soon as he saw her approaching the counter, he sluggishly stood up and reappeared to direct her to the visitor's room.

"Hey! Munchkin!" Margie acclaimed on seeing Molly. Molly's excitement knew no bounds at the sight of her. But, the transparent glass noticeably formed a barrier between the two. Their smiles drooped for a while as they couldn't hug each other. The hope that lit their smiles once more is that, they are seeing each other. Molly smiled back again as she placed her palm against the glass and Margie quickly smiled back as she matched her palm to Molly's.

They drew closer to the glass and hastened with the pleasantries bearing in mind the duration of their meeting. Noticing Molly's obvious thrills, Margie became weary in breaking the most awful news she would want to hear at the moment. Her vagueness quickly drew Molly's attention to inquiringly ask, "Are you ok?"

"No…Yes," she ostentatiously stammered to Molly's discernment. The snoopy stare Molly fixed on her for a while motioned her to let the cat out of the bag.

"Alright… I'm not fine," she gloomily said as she rose up her shoulders a bit simultaneously. As she took her time to structure her words, Molly's grievous anticipation for the news became intolerable.

"What?" She curiously asked as she drew more closely to the glass, awakening Margie's vagueness. Margie drew closer to ensure they have the contact needed to handle what she has to say.

"Alright," she managed to say and gently wetted her lips and flipped her hair behind her right ear in order to buy herself more time. "Molly, whatever I'm going to say now should not tear you apart in any way please," she pleaded as Molly nodded in affirmation and she weakly continued. "Molly, Robin… will be buried today," Margie finally added in clear sympathy.

Molly's facial expression changed immediately, "what?"

"Molly, please pull yourself together."

Molly slowly bowed down her head in anguish as tears gently narrowed down her cheeks unceasingly. She gruesomely grabbed her orange colored shirt by the chest, squeezed it forcefully and she cried in severe pain. As her shoulders jerked to her sniffs, so did sweat drip down from her skull down to her chest and all over. Her sorrow heightened intensively that she could not notice Margie's consolatory words.

Instantly, the police officer barged into the room unannounced as Ginika stood inertly behind him. Margie grasped her handkerchief tightly to her face and wiped her tears as the police officer asked her out. Ginika pleaded with him for Margie not to leave but he declined her request.

Just as Margie made her way out, Molly raised her reddened face and spoke up amidst tears to their surprise. "I believe you are my lawyer," she said referring to Ginika and the three stood still.

"Yes, I am Ginika Emechelu. I'm here to thrash out this case with you; I mean to know what really happened."

"There will be no need for that," Molly added to their amazement. Then she stood up and concluded meanly as she sniffed uncontrollably. "My story is already famous. The only thing you should know is that… I didn't kill my only brother." She uttered as she mumbled with tears. "Please, do me a favor, attend my brother's funeral with Margie and pay him the last respect on my behalf," she requested humbly.

"Please… I," Ginika tried to chip in as she walked out.

"I think she needs some space," the police officer kindly advised to tie up the discussion.

Molly's drowsy movement alerted Olivia, and then she quickly stood up and wrapped her hands round the poles of her cell. She watched closely as Molly staggered to her cell. Her sorrowful cry ignited her tender emotions and she calmly asked, "Dear friend, what's wrong?"

Molly tried to control her tears as she helplessly sat down on the floor but her perceived doomed nature and love for her late brother increased the torments within her, leaving her with no choice than to cry more.

After a while of silence, Molly unexpectedly began talking inaudibly.

"*Amidst all troubles dear one…,*

keep calm and know I'm here." Olivia listened keenly, as she discovered its Kiosk's song; she slowly knelt down on her juvenile knees and joined Molly in her grief-stricken chant,

"*if the trouble's rage gets tougher*

quickly whisper to the nearest cool breeze

I miss you dear," they sang sadly as tears majestically stumbled down their jaws in drips.

"*be calm my dear for just in a jiffy*

ripples of my love for you

will come directly to your heart

to adorn you with peace

absolute peace, so be calm my dear for I'm here

So be calm my dear for I'm here" they ended the song with grievous sniffs.

Olivia clearly understood what the song was meant for when Molly exhaustedly said, "Robin my brother will be buried today and I won't be going." Olivia swiftly wiped tears off her eyes with her soft palms and sympathetically asserted

"That's heartbreaking; I am really sorry dear friend. You know, granny once told me that…" and she knelt erect to explain her self-indulgent idea gotten from granny's stories as Molly gently looked to her direction.

"Our beloved ones who we couldn't attend their funerals will always forgive us whenever we strike our left breast sincerely and declare - *death isn't an excuse, my genuine love for you prevails at all times-* Unbelievably, each time I do this I feel at peace with myself," she narrated with innocent smile and added, "Would you mind to give it a try?"

"No," Molly replied as they hurriedly stood up, and declared in loud voices while striking their left breasts. "Death isn't an excuse; my genuine love for you prevails at all times."

Obviously, those words were tranquility to the soul as it was evident in Molly's sudden litheness. Olivia felt so fulfilled and explained calmly. "I always do that whenever I miss my mom."

"This is indeed divine. I feel so relieved right now. Thank you so much," Molly gladly acknowledged.

"I'm glad you are comforted," she replied with enormous joy

of fulfillment as she winged her arms sideways.

Few people who could attend the impromptu funeral came with sadness and anger. They grieved for the loss and their anger was directed to Susan. All that came were in attendance for Molly and Robin. Indeed, Robin would know that death isn't an excuse.

Robin's burial didn't stop the city's busy schedule or the court hearing the next day. Moreover, he was an average youth without notable achievements to reckon on. Susan's vengeance for her son's spontaneous death stirred up in her negligence to courtesy. Friends and well wishers expected her to take her time to mourn her son but inversely, she went to the court hearing.

All she desires is to daringly watch Doctor Larry and his team; Mr. Douglas and Molly

spend the rest of their lives in jail. Her optimism obviously led her bold footsteps into the court room.

Her vehement lawyer is seated with her right leg crossed over the other. Her relaxed mood clearly shows in her hands directly on her crossed knees. Her knee length, Vixcos brand, dark red colored gown declared her doggedness up to her directly fixed neck which portrayed her classy gold necklace. Her dark red lipstick is out with its function to match with her gown. The blonde hair she bears gave a deciding factor to her valiant beauty. Obviously, she is ready to do her job perfectly well as usual.

Susan softly patted Vanessa's shoulder to draw her attention behind her. The majestic turn she took to depict her class visibly presented her self-importance. The brief exchange of pleasantries plainly announced to Susan that she needed sometime to herself. As he turned, Susan took a deep breath of confidence in her lawyer's Venomic power. She looked around the court in amazement to how well organized the court room is.

The cleaners plainly did a good job with the sparkling floor, dazzling tables, chairs and rails, incredibly arranged files, astounding curtain designs in their spectacular positions, magenta scented air freshener which gave the room its pleasant smell and the glittering white painted ceiling. All of these formed a contributing entity to the unique nature of the room.

Instantaneously, her eye caught up with Molly's entrance. She stared mutely in pity with a mother's love for her daughter written all over face as Molly walked in with handcuff fitted to her wrists. Nature has a way of holding its subjects captive with emotions.

Susan's rigid conscience speedily melted in accordance to her daughter's miserable condition. Molly took a glance at her but Susan quickly looked away because she couldn't stand the guilty she felt inwardly.

Ginika gently entered with Margie and Charles. Margie caught sight of Douglas at the right end but couldn't reach to him due to strict restrictions placed on the culprits. Her compassion for his state grew on noticing his calm status. As she wondered why he seemed so undisturbed, unexpectedly, the court's clerk gave an order for all to rise.

The judge regally walked in as all in the court arouse in respect to his legal status. The courtroom's door was shut as all sat in anticipation of the outcome of what is on deck.

The judge extensively explained the notion of the case to the court and summoned the plaintiff to take over the already recognized protocol.

Vanessa stood up and walked up to the stage courageously, as she began speaking with all confidence, instantly, Gozax Internal Bureau Intelligence (GIBI) officers were ushered in with a legal permit. The court inhabitants anxiously watched them as they matched towards the judge's desk. Vanessa promptly stopped on noticing the distracted gestures made by the audience.

Their curious gazes vividly wondered what GIBI officers would be doing in the courtroom. The officers pulled out their IDs one after the other on getting to the judge to reveal their origin. Then the judge loudly apologized to the court and requested for few minutes with the officers. The officer in front who seems to be in charge spoke inaudibly with the judge and handed over a file he bore to him.

Vanessa gently took some steps back to her seat, as she waited anxiously with her elbow pointing on her desk and both of her hands directly under her jaw, the judge curiously pulled out the content of the file in his hand. His facial expression became gloomy on comprehending the major information on the paper he has. He swiftly redressed on his seat, grabbed his phone and dialed it with so much unease.

After a while of conversation on phone, he hung up and redressed again to address the court.

CHAPTER NINETEEN

The miraculous intervention

"The government has bought the Molly Chopkin's project," he stated and paused sequel to the immediate tantrum it raised in the court. While the side talks from the witnesses took time to diminish at the clerk's order for silence, Vanessa tried to wrap her mind round the hidden aim of the government as Susan quickly sat up in fury.

"In that case," the judge continued in earnest. "This case is here by officially dismissed; the culprits will be taken by these officers to city's special science research center in Radmay district."

"What?" Vanessa angrily said with a squeezed face of humiliation.

"I am really sorry for the inconvenience," the judge concluded and slammed the court's hammer on its slate and stood up to leave on the clerk's order. "Court!"

The officers instantly headed for Molly, Douglas, doctor Larry and his team as the witnesses arose chattering their opinions as they left. The officers hoarded them into their van and drove off in a jiffy.

Vanessa rushed out immediately in order to have a chat with the judge. As Susan waited patiently for her outside the courtroom, Ginika, Margie and Charles emerged and tried to start up a conversation but were rudely interrupted.

"I guess your complexion concurs to bribery, black lawyer," Susan insolently muttered to their surprise. "What!" Margie acclaimed meanly. "Madam, be careful with your words," Ginika warned and walked away as Margie and Charles calmly followed suit.

Few hours later, Vanessa came out with a long face and explained to Susan that nothing can be done. She drove home with so much grief and shame. It is a huge loss and a stinky spat on the face. Instead of driving home, she headed to Eric's house to cry out her eyes.

GIBI's miraculous intervention dwelled in Molly's mind as they drove to the research center. She diligently meditated on the turns of inevitable facts Vanessa could have presented against her and her miserable fate after judgment.

She gently rubbed her palms together and pushed it in between her knees making her bow her head a bit. Just then a feeling of victory and slim escape from a hunter's trap struck her. She sluggishly raised her head, resting it against the van and puffed out some air from her lungs in relief.

"We should be worried about what the intervener wants from us," Douglas chipped in quietly with a matured glance at her on noticing her restlessness. Molly's side gaze reminded her that she is just seeing Douglas after so many weeks. The she released herself from the van on which she rested.

"You know, I have missed you rosary man?" She drolly complimented with smiles. "I have missed you too, child," Douglas replied with smiles and they drew closer to each other for a warm embrace. In a tick, they loosed hold of each other to discuss what is ahead of them.

"Do you think the government has a hidden agenda?" Molly asked with so much concern in her facial appearance. Just then the van stopped its movement. As they heard the doors open Douglas quickly replied almost inaudibly, "We would know when we get there."

As they walked into the research building, Molly felt a bit liberal although she doesn't know what their goal is in the

research center but at least her hands were no longer cuffed.

The corridors in the building were flanked by laboratories which are enormously sophisticated with equipment of several capacities. Some of the researchers in the labs noticed them and wondered why they came while the others were a bit busy to notice them.

The officer who led them briefly opened the door to one of the labs and ushered them in. Molly took her time to look around sensitively and hastily noticed that the white bulbs in the lab made it almost impossible for one to see the most insignificant thing that drops on the floor.

"Sir, here are the culprits from the cloning case," the officer initiated an introduction between them and the scientist they just met.

"Oh! Wow, that's great," the scientist acclaimed with bold smiles while Molly drew closer to rest her body on one of the steel like shelves directly by her side with experimental bottles all over it.

"This is Mr. Douglas," the officer muttered, directing his right index finger towards Douglas. "It's my pleasure to meet you Douglas," the scientist commented as they shook hands. "And this is Molly, the owner of the project," the officer interrupted sharply.

"That's great, nice to meet you Molly," the scientist said with a wave of hello. "Same here," Molly replied.

"Molly, Douglas this is Mr. Richard in charge of biological and natural researches here," the officer asserted as they nodded. "I will leave you with him now. Feel relaxed, he will give you further explanations you need," he concluded and took few steps backwards to leave.

"Thank you so much officer," Douglas appreciated sincerely as they shook hands. "You are welcome," the officer replied and walked away. Mr. Richard commenced his briefing when he noticed he had their full attention.

"You are welcome once again," he said. "Thank you," they chorused in unison.

He offered them seats opposite his desk and sat on his chair directly behind the desk. He gently reduced the table lamp's brightness, rested his arm on the desk and began explaining the cause of their sudden arrival to the city's research institute.

"Few days ago, your cloning trial came to the President's knowledge through one of the city's newspapers. He contacted us, inquiring if this institute is aware of such trial but we declined because truly we knew nothing about it.

His astonishment for such an intense biological manipulation prompted him to conduct investigations concerning the cloning. From its origin till date," He paused and adjusted on his seat as they listened keenly.

"When he realized you all involved in the failed cloning trial will be charged to court today he decided to take over the case. Compensations have been allotted for all collateral damages including your brother's death. He intends to use the cloning project as a scheme to fight for Xylom Limestone," he diligently detailed. "What?" Molly muttered without thinking.

"Sorry, I need to understand this," Douglas quickly said with confusion as he scratched the tip of his right ear with his right hand. "Ok," Richard answered in anticipation of his question.

"You stated that compensation has been made for Robin's death?" He asked inquisitively, "Yes" Richard replied promisingly. "How much?" he asked again without hesitating.

"I do not know but it has been put in place. I guess it will be paid directly into your mother's account," he answered referring to Molly as Molly and Douglas took a quick stare at each other.

"What of Doctor Larry and his team?" Molly asked caringly as she drew her seat closer to the desk.

"They have been set free, including you Mr. Douglas but with a ban from service for eight years," he smiled pitifully.

"The President has no right to do that," Douglas interrupted scrupulously while he sat up on his seat.

"*Hahaha,*" Richard laughed out and continued. "That is exactly what power can do. Coupled with the fact that we are in a society where anything goes."

"Hmm," Douglas breathed out heavily. "And Molly?" He asked as Molly swiftly sat up on hearing her name.

"She is now an employee in this institute but with restricted movements. She will be residing at the GIBI estate and will be coming to work from there," Richard answered to their amazement. "I will…" he continued but was stridently interrupted

"Sorry, for how long is she going to work with those terms," Douglas worriedly asked.

"For seven years, like I was about to say. The details are contained in a contract to be signed by you and your lawyers in two days," he momentarily explained as they kept mute. Richard noticed their coldness and quickly broke the silence.

"I mean it's a two way something, either a lifetime in jail or this offer. You choose," Richard jokingly chipped in.

"Please can I spend the night with my friend Margie, and then come with my lawyer on the next day?" Molly requested meekly.

"I don't think that will be possible, the GIBI officer is waiting for you outside," he replied to their astonishment. "Wow!" she mumbled inwardly.

"Cheer up my dear, you will be fine," Douglas consoled as he squeezed her right shoulder. "We would be on our way now," he said as they stood to leave.

"Thanks for the briefing," he added as they shook hand again. "You are welcome," Richard replied as they made their way to the door quietly.

Molly and Douglas bided goodbye with a mutual plan for Molly to go in search of Picasso. Her travel permit was granted with duration of two weeks. Having concluded the dual signing of their agreement with the government, she made her way to Losuzy city in search of Picasso's findings which may help her project significantly.

It took few days to locate his previous residence. Unfortunately, she met with the most inappropriate news she wanted.

"Picasso is dead. He passed on like 7 to 8 months ago," the shabby looking old man she approached announced to her in a manner of uncertainty with the timing. "But, I'm sure he is dead," he added immediately without giving Molly a chance to react to the unexpected news.

"Hope all is well?" He probed on noticing Molly gloomy absenteeism. "Are you Picasso's …" He curiously solicited again but was cut short by Molly's hasty inquiry. "Please what killed him?"

Then he adjusted indolently backwards on his seat and answered devastatingly, "He died of heart failure."

Molly took few steps backwards in disappointments as her aim of coming to Losuzy was panning out in crumbles. "I always cautioned his heavy drinking and incessant smoking, but he didn't listen," the stranger added innocently to lighten the situation.

Molly stood helplessly with her hands on her waist. As she took a dawdling look at the old-fashioned house before her, it unexpectedly struck her mind to interrogate him a bit. Then hastily she took few steps forward, pulled out her back bag and sat down on a cemented pavement close to the stranger.

"How close were you with Picasso?" she silently questioned. "He was a good friend, we, we …watched football together. Although, he always advised I should quit watching football because of my high blood pressure, but I couldn't because it makes me happy," he muttered with genuine laughter. "He was family; we played board cheese, cooked together…"

"Did he ever mention any cloning research to you," Molly inquired anxiously."A cloning research?" He asked haggardly with dimmed eyes of confusion. "Yes, a cloning research," Molly replied strongly as he turned his eyes upwards and back fort to remember if there was any. But the process was interrupted by Molly's impatient curiosity.

"The cloning research his friend Donald started," Molly quickly chipped in to hasten the memory recall process. "Oh! Yes, he did mention Donald," he declared with bold smiles to Molly's gladness. "But, he didn't mention a cloning research," he quickly added. "What?" Molly asked with dismay. "He didn't mention it but gave me a huge file for anybody that comes in search of him," he reported weakly.

"Can I see the file please" Molly requested meekly with her palms clumped together to her chest "No, I can't do that," he replied to her surprise. "I don't know you," he rightly added and adjusted again.

"Ok," Molly said and took a deep breath. "I am Molly, Donald's daughter. I took up the cloning research recently but I needed some information from Picasso which may be contained in that file if you would allow me see it."

After so much pleading, the old chap took his time to ascertain Molly's candor before handing over the file to her. She appreciated him sincerely and made her way back to Gozax the same day.

The file literally deprived her of sleep; she kept on digging for valuable information contained in the parcel until she got to the last paper. Then she took a deep breath, lifted the table lamp shining directly on her face and took a glance at the wall clock directly opposite her bed.

It was 3:06am to her astonishment, she yawned heavily and lazily uttered, "Thank you, Picasso." Then she fell into her bed and dozed off.

The first knock on her door seemed like a drum beat in her dream, as seconds went by into minutes, she speedily jumped up from her slumber when the knock upgraded into a bang. Obviously, the pounding sound reached her ears from her door.

"Who is that?" She angrily inquired without getting a reply as her legs double crossed each other to the door and forcefully opened it.

"I was sleeping and not in coma!" She instantly yelled at the young lad standing before her but got a cute cool smile from him. "I don't think so," he replied still smiling. "I have been knocking for half an hour now. I wouldn't doubt you were in coma," he added now with mild laughter but didn't get same approach from Molly.

"Why are you smiling and why are you here?" She asked spitefully as she crossed her arms underneath her breast making the knocker's smiles to fade gently.

"Oh!" He said on noticing her spiteful mood. "Firstly, I was smiling not for the sake of a good morning but because I'm so much aware that you do not know the state of your hair right now," he stated looking funnily at her jumbled hair. Molly slowly pushed her eyes upwards towards her forehead to verify what he is talking about but he quickly interrupted to announce why he came. "The president is here to see you."

"What!" She shockingly shouted with her eyes wide open like that of a frog and sharply slammed the door on his face. "I will be waiting," he declared with a high tune hoping she would hear him. Molly quickly brushed her teeth, washed her face and dashed out still in her night dress

"What are you wearing?" He surprisingly inquired with a confused face. "Let's go please," Molly carelessly answered after looking sharply at herself. "No way, please go and change. Skip the part that you just woke up, trust me you are going to work," he calmly requested and she rushed back into her room again.

"If possible put on a makeup," he candidly advised as she slammed the door to his face again.

Clearly the president had waited impatiently for them to arrive at the research institute. Officially, it isn't right to keep him waiting but his desperate nature for a new strategy against Boathabs deprived him of exercising his Presidential rights to its full length. A little query settled the case and the meeting commenced.

The meeting comprised of the president, Mr. Richard (Head of Biological and natural resources), the Chief of Army staff, Molly and other distinguished scientists and personalities. Molly rendered a detailed report from the genesis of the cloning project till date and her findings from Picasso's research.

The meeting uncovered strange biological manipulations they never knew existed. Apparently, all they anxiously await is the commencement of the scheme in order to witness the greatest scientific discovery of the century. Prolifically, they carefully selected special animal subjects they would want to use based on Molly's findings and scheduled for immediate serum collection.

Additionally, the board decided to put up an invitation to soldiers who would want to be used for the cloning scheme. The meeting ended with multidimensional expectations from the government, the scientists and Molly.

Molly walked majestically with so much self fulfillment. In no time, the institute was filled with details about her project. As she walked down the long corridor, unfamiliar workers threw greetings at her to her surprise.

"I can see you feel so great this morning," the officer who brought her whispered to her with beam. "Of course it is," she answered amidst happiness.

The cool breeze that slammed into her on her way out illuminated the gladness within her the more. Her steps became more distinct as her smiles led her way. "Congratulations," the officer quickly chipped in as he opened the car for her. "Thank you," she said and joyfully entered the car.

"No. 24 Mamieu-Beet," Molly hastily said as soon as the officer sat on the driver's seat. "Ok ma," he funnily replied as he carefully brought out the car key from his pocket and lunched it into the car's ignition point.

It was a smooth ride to Mr. Douglas's residence. His joy knew no bounds when he beheld Molly stepping out of the car. He quickly stood up and waved to her from his balcony and she responded with a shaky wave out of joy. Douglas perceived her lithe mood and dashed into his sitting room to grab a bottle of wine.

On his sudden disappearance, Molly turned to the officer and jokingly asked, "Would you mind to join us or wait here, Mr. Smiles?"

His outburst in laughter conjoined with hers for a while, "Really, Mr. Smiles?" He replied amidst laughter. "Yeah, you did not tell me you name. So?"

"I didn't tell because you didn't ask," he strongly defended but still broke Molly's few seconds of muteness. "I'm Lucas, do not worry I already know yours," he out rightly declared and they burst into laughter again.

Molly quickly swung her handbag into her left hand and stretched it out for a handshake, "Nice to meet you, Lucas."

"Same here, I will be in charge of your parole while it lasts in GIBI," he added shortly before their hands went loose and Molly made her way to the stairs.

"Oh! So I am now a GIBI officer or agent?" she asked teasingly as she took her time with the stairs. "GIBI agent will be preferable," he answered but was sharply stopped by Molly's sudden turn to him. "Why agent and not officer," she asked with utmost seriousness to his bewilderment.

"Uhmm, can I see your badge please," he requested solely but got silent strange stares with an unidentified feeling locked within it from her. "Get lost," Molly ordered sparingly amidst laughter as she turned and headed for the sitting room.

CHAPTER TWENTY

Similarities – Genetic lock up

The atmosphere assumed a party like one on Margie's entrance. Molly summoned her to join them as they haven't had such a good time in a while. The reunion was a fun filled one. They seem to have been reunited from exiles. Their joy escalated to Lucas and to everything within the four corners of the sitting room. Suddenly, Molly became gloomy as Douglas and Margie enjoyed their laughter.

"What's wrong?" Lucas curiously asked to their hearing. Their laughter ceased immediately so did the atmosphere change as well.

"I miss Robin," she sadly muttered as she held her glass of wine loosely. Douglas took a deep breath and slacked backwards on the cushion on which he sat. Margie gently placed her glass on the side stool by her side and bowed her head understandingly.

"I miss his defenses, company, loud music and of course the fights," she stated painfully as Douglas slowly rested his neck backwards making his head to face up. The cloning trial began playing vividly in his head.

Robin's exact words at death stroke him differently this time. *"I'm sorry, I'm passing out,"* then he closed his eyes tenderly in deep pains.

"I don't know Robin," Lucas interrupted. "But I believe he was a good man and indeed will be proud of you wherever he is," he solemnly encouraged. Then raised his glass and cheered, "To Robin!" in unison they all slowly raised their glasses and replied, "To Robin."

Douglas sullenly emptied the wine in his mouth, took some time to push it down his throat and looked up to Molly. "How did it go with Picasso?"

"Picasso is dead," she answered as she drew closer to the center table. "What!" Margie shouted in surprise. "Who is Picasso?" Lucas ignorantly asked.

"He is my dad's friend who took up the cloning project when he passed on," she replied him and continued.

"Luckily, I met his friend who gave me a file he left behind. The file kept me up till this morning. The findings aren't funny but are negotiable," she stated but their confusion heightened with her last statement which prompted Margie to ask,

"How do you mean, not funny but negotiable?"

"Picasso discovered that somatic gene differs in organisms, such that man's somatic gene of walking is hopping in frog and talking in man is bleats in goats and so on but somatic cell division is similar in all organisms except in the reproductive system that two daughter cells are produced. Now, because of the similarity in the somatic cell division; a genetic lock up occurs when somatic fluids of organisms with similarities are cloned," she extensively explained to their understanding yet she got no reply but nods then she continued.

"Organisms with similarities include: man, fox, dog, chimpanzee, whale, dolphin and so on. When any two of these animals I mentioned are been cloned, their somatic genes rapidly divides and conjoins with each other in a lock up manner because of their similarities. Instantly, they begin to understand their genes as one divide as one and lock up into one because of their similarities. When a genetic lock up occurs, it's almost impossible to change to unlock with the mind. He also noted that the greatest genetic lock up is seen when paired with fox, then dog and chimpanzee," she explained further to their clarity.

"Are there any experimental back up for this?" Lucas interrupted immediately in curiosity. "Yes, he attached pictures of failed trials in the file. Painfully, his adopted son died as a result of one of his cloning trials," she sadly announced.

"So, in essence?" Douglas wisely asked. Molly kept still for a while because she understood what Douglas's question meant and then retorted sorrowfully.

"I suspect Robin accidentally died of the same case. The percentage of the dog's somatic fluid used was much higher than the others."

Douglas regrettably puffed out some air from his mouth in sadness. But the deed had already been done. Then Margie quickly asked, "What's the negotiable part?"

"Such similar organisms can be avoided completely or can be used moderately and with caution. Other animals such as lions, tigers, cheetahs and cats can also be used."

"A quick one, so what's the difference between the genetic nature of a lion and a dog?" Lucas intelligently asked.

"Lion is known just for its strength and boldness. Dog has all that namely: fastness, perseverance, sense of smell, compassion, empathy, even strength and boldness. So, it makes lion safer to use. Fox is more risky because of its wild nature. Apparently, it belongs to the dog's family. He also hypothesized that a dog's somatic gene can be used for a cripple," she answered but was inquisitively interrupted by Lucas and Margie in unison. "A cripple?"She nodded.

"Is the government fully aware of this?" Douglas questioned interestedly with a fixed stare on her.

"Of course," she asserted strongly. "I detailed all these to them a while ago and they accepted the circumstances and carefully accepted their animal subjects for cloning."

"Is there any kind of antidote or something, if eventually something goes wrong?" Margie curiously asked with freight.

"None for now," she replied hopelessly as she shook her head sideways. "This is indeed deadly," Margie concluded coldly.

"Who are the human subjects?" Lucas quickly inquired. "Soldiers."

"Soldiers?" Lucas surprisingly asked with his eyes looking up to her. "Yes, soldiers," she responded and made her way to the refrigerator.

"Wow!" He acclaimed happily. "Then, I am your first subject," he asserted strongly to their surprise. "Really?" Margie said.

"Yes, I will do it," he generously volunteered. "I'm grateful," Molly appreciated still holding onto the pack of juice she brought out from the refrigerator.

Douglas uttered no word to Lucas' decision. The quick stare he threw at him walked down his thoughts to Lucas but he ignored it just like Robin did out of enthusiasm.

As Molly opened the pack of juice and poured some directly into her mouth, Douglas stated

"Molly, there's one more thing,"

"What?" Molly asked and swallowed the juice at a snail's pace and sat down calmly.

"I spoke with Doctor Larry yesterday and he…"

"And he said what?" Margie quickly interrupted

"He disclosed to me that Robin… he said Robin had hard drugs in his blood stream" he finally stated and the others

relaxed a bit as he didn't say what they expected

"How?" Molly asked

"The autopsy was completed. The lumpy substances that were found in his blood vessels were tested and proven to be hard drugs. He also confirmed he had been into it for long time such that it has started weakening his internal organs. The one that was found in his blood vessels is the one that he took just before the cloning trial"

"It's true," Molly bluntly stated "Mom, was right. She had noticed it and complained to me but I doubted her. I also remember that day of the trial, I excused myself for a while and before I could come back, I didn't see him. I waited for him, after some time; he emerged from the rest room. I thought he went to ease himself or something…" she affirmed and breathed out heavily

"I checked the CCTV camera in my lab and it showed he

took it in the rest room probably because he was tensed." He said and the others remained calm

"Robin didn't die through your cloning trial Molly. When his activity level increased due to cloning specimens that was injected into him, the heart pumped blood at a very high rate which the blocked veins couldn't carry, and that resulted to a high blood pressure and a heart attack," Douglas explained

"Hmm, did he why there was a high activity level?" Lucas asked

"The activity level increased because he was asked to make a lot of demonstrations and still changed to human afterwards. Better still, he would have being able to carry the rate of increase if his blood vessels were free," Douglas answered and Molly breathed out

"I still miss you Robin," Molly said softly

Douglas openly advised, "Molly I think you should go and see your mother."

"She wouldn't want to see me, not to talk of what happened in court," she briefly lamented with an overcast face. "Just give it a try," Douglas spurred.

"Ok, I will," she said sluggishly in acceptance and poured in the juice into her mouth again.

The last time she saw her residence, she was in handcuffs and tears of hopelessness. The environs seemed clearly abandoned. The flowers had exceeded their boundaries and the cleaner seemed to be on strike. Absolutely, something was different. She took a deep breath right in front of the door before pressing its bell.

She could hear Susan's weak voice from the inside ushering her into the house. She gently looked back at Lucas who stood by the car waiting and he nodded encouraging her to take the brave step.

She stepped into the house to find her mother lying helplessly on the floor. She took a flashy move to her, pulled her up and began questioning her but got no immediate reply. Susan's vulnerable state divested her of unleashing her anger on Molly.

Just then she muttered faintly. "Prisca tried to…" then she coughed out uncontrollably. "Prisca tried to do what?" Molly worriedly asked in fear of losing her mother.

"To strangle me to death," she weakly added still coughing. "What!" Molly exclaimed angrily in disappointment. "Please save me, please," Susan hopelessly whispered to her ears as her eyes began closing.

"Mom, mom!" Molly yelled in great panic. She quickly reached out for Lucas' help and they conveyed her to the hospital.

Molly sat exhaustedly at the hospital's waiting room. Her mind roamed about what her mother had told her earlier. Apparently lost in thought, Lucas calmly interrupted with a cup of coffee to bring her back to reality.

"Oh! Thank you," she nostalgically said as she received the cup of coffee. "Are you alright?" Lucas caringly ascertained while he sat down. "Not really," she replied worriedly and took a sip from the cup of coffee.

"What's wrong?" He questioned with intent stares at her.

"My mom whispered to me that her friend tried to strangle her," she mumbled almost inaudibly into his left ear. "What? That's serious," Lucas said.

"Yeah, I can't just wrap my head around it," she stated with dim facial expression and continued, "because the person in question is her best friend."

"Wow!" Lucas exclaimed and took a sip from the cup of coffee. "I suggest we should ensure she is fine then go check out the cameras."

"That's a point, but can you do me a favor?" Molly chipped in and turned to him directly. "What?"

"Please help me check out the cameras while I remain here with her because someone can break into the house and tamper with the evidence if there is any," she softly requested.

"I'm really sorry, I can't leave you. That's the order I'm working with but I can call my friend Jamil…" he replied and she turned immediately in dissatisfaction.

"Don't worry he is my best friend, I trust him," he added believably. "Are you sure?"

"Yes," he assured. "Let me quickly call him," he added as he straightened his right leg and slot his hand into his pocket to get his phone.

Susan was revived few hours later. In her helpless state she breathed through a tiny wire like pipe connected to her nostrils to supply oxygen. She dimly breathed in and out, as a result her strength longed for a recharge. The normal saline went in drips into the tiny pipe connected directly to her intracellular veins to energize her.

She soothingly opened her eyes as soon as Lucas stepped in first and Molly proceeded. Molly's nonchalant steps towards the foot of the bed evidently showed how terrified she is to see her mother. Susan glued her intently bound dim stares on her as she stood still by her foot.

Their quietude seemed endless as they both lacked words to express their piled up feelings. Lucas was about breaking the silence when Susan weakly stretched out her right hand beckoning on Molly to their surprise.

Unprecedented tears hastily wetted her eyeballs as she saw her mother's reaction and quickly responded to it. She dropped her handbag on the trolley that stood by the bed and speedily grabbed her hand.

"I'm truly sorry mom," she softly muttered with remorse and tears paced down her cheeks. Susan kept mute for a while in soreness wondering what to say to her daughter.

"I can't reject you forever, Molly," she uttered slowly in low tone as Molly still cried. "But you are my child, my only daughter. No matter how much hatred I have for you Molly, you remain my only surviving child."

"I strongly believe that Robin never wanted things to play out this way but sadly it happened and I'm super proud of him. My strong desire to obtain justice for him almost cost my own life," she stated sniffing uncontrollably. "I am so sorry for the pains I caused you."

"It is ok mom. Save yourself some strength," Molly caringly advised and hugged her tightly. "Thank you for saving my

life," Susan added as they still held each other.

They let go of themselves only to notice someone had walked in on their sorrowful moment without their notice. Molly quickly turned to Lucas with curious gawks. He comprehended the strange look on her face and quickly introduced the unknown friend.

"Forgive me," he briefly apologized. "This is my friend that I asked to check out the cameras."

"Oh!" Molly softly acclaimed with relief.

"Jam, please meet Molly," Lucas succinctly introduced. Jamil friendly shook hands with her and waved to Susan whom he couldn't reach to because of her condition.

"Did you find anything?" Molly anxiously inquired to his surprise but was prompted by Lucas to go on with his report. He took a deep breath to relax his nerves and brought out his phone from his pocket.

"I checked all the cameras both inside and outside the house," he acknowledged as he tried to on his phone. "Luckily, the camera in the sitting room directly captured a strange woman who tried to strangle her."

"That was Prisca," Susan quickly chipped in with confidence. "Are you sure?" Molly ascertained as she turned to her. "Yes, she was the one," Susan confirmed as Jamil handed over the phone to Lucas to play the video and Susan continued.

"She is jealously angry for my affairs with Eric," Susan explained feebly but was rudely interrupted by Molly. "Oh, Robin was right huh?"

"Yes he was but I needed someone in my life that I could be affectionately close with. Unfortunately, Robin found out before I could disclose it to any of you," she shamefully narrated

"I have been at his house after the court visit. Few hours after I returned to the house, Prisca barged into the house with so much fury and began lamenting on…" she asserted but was cut short by an intense cough.

"It's ok mom. Please have some rest," Molly kindly advised as she caressed her chest to stop the cough. Lucas played the video and handed over the phone to Molly to confirm if the woman in the video is Prisca.

Jamil breathed out heavily as Molly confirmed affirmatively to the video. "I think it is wise for me to leave this district for now," Susan quickly chipped in to break the silence. "To where?" Molly nervously questioned.

"To Stockazul, Karen's place," she answered. "I think she should be relocated to another place even if it's against medical advice," Jamil firmly suggested and continued as the others directed their eyes at him. "I noticed a gang of lads went into that house as I was driving out. I couldn't go after them because I was unarmed. Moreover, I deleted all evidence the cameras had."

"Molly, do we have your approval on this? It seems this should be done as soon as possible," Lucas interestedly asked with his hands in his pocket. "Yes, let's do it," Molly strongly confirmed to Susan's relief.

They summoned the doctor in charge and clearly stated their plan to him. After much persuasion to make them change their minds seemed abortive, he innocently handed over the *discharge against medical advice form* to Molly to fill and sign.

Molly contacted Karen (Susan's younger sister) before Susan's flight took off. She pleaded with Karen to pick her from the airport and not to disclose Susan's where about to anyone no matter what.

Molly and the lads drove back to the GIBI estate as soon as Susan's flight took off. The contagious happiness that filled the estate was enormous. There was so much drinking, food, loud music, clashes of cheering glasses and laughter from different corners of the estate.

"What's happening?" Molly inquisitively asked with unfocused stares to and fro as she stepped down from the car.

"Today is Mamieu's day," Jamil gladly informed with bold smiles as he was already adapting to the change in the atmosphere.

"That's true," Molly shamefully retorted because she totally forgot one of her memorable days in the city. Shortly, Jamil sighted one of his friends and bided them goodbye with warm hugs.

"No wonder Mr. Douglas offered us wine, unlike him," she meditatively thought as she walked down up to Lucas. "What's your plan for the celebration in the air?" Lucas inquired with smiles.

"Uhmm…" Molly momentarily brain stormed for any idea but got none. "Nothing, I will enter my room, lock the door, take my bath and sleep. It has been a long day."

"Such plan is a flop for one of Gozax's special days, come on!" Lucas commented in disappointment.

"Its Gozax's special day, not mine," Molly answered and took a step forward.

"Every moment of our lives is special if we make it so. Oh my God! You are making me poetic" He said stressfully and Molly smirked dubiously without saying a word.

"Ok, shift ends by 7pm. How about I help you get another permit so that we can visit Mamieu Fun Park later tonight and watch the fireworks. I'm sure, you know the celebration tastes different at that spot," he carefully requested.

"I'm in," Molly affirmed laughing. "Yes!" Lucas strongly acclaimed as though he had won a lottery ticket, "I will call you soonest. Go and get ready while I work out your permit."

Molly joyfully took her bath. Presently, not because it's Mamieu's day but for reasons she couldn't grab with her hand. Her beauty waxed enormously due to unadulterated gladness that emanated from within. With her case, one can bring to a close that indeed happiness is a true framework to beauty.

She took her time to sing along side her preparation. Her mood was lithe. As she pulled down her gown through her head, it quickly struck her that she hadn't called Douglas or Margie since they parted ways earlier in the day.

She hurriedly pushed her hands into the sleeves one after the other and took some strides to her table. She pulled out the chair and sat down as the calm musical notes still emits from her lips.

She untied her dough knotted hair, waggled it about and picked up her phone. She dialed the numbers she had in mind but none picked her calls.

"Probably, they are at the fun park," she thought freely and made her way to the mirror. "But Douglas wouldn't be at the fun park," she briefly thought again but now worriedly. She picked up her phone and dialed his number again but got no reply.

Suddenly, Lucas barged in without a knock and she quickly turned to him. "I'm almost ready" Molly politely said, he replied with lively nods and sat down on the bed.

"Douglas and Margie aren't picking their calls," she restlessly reported. "They may be busy with something," he suggested still sitting. "But, Douglas never misses his calls for anything," Molly anxiously lamented and then Lucas stood up and walked up to her

saying, "Then, he broke the record today."

He hastily continued as his little joke could not calm her disturbed mind, "Look," he added holding her arm and she looked into his eyes silently. "You worry too much Molly. I understand you have been through a whole lot recently, but that shouldn't give a room for easy negative thoughts. They are fine" She nodded scarcely in relief. "Now, dress up lets go," Lucas courteously ordered and she turned to the mirror and continued with her dressing.

She was ready in few minutes and they were ready to go. Her phone rang as she opened her purse to put it, it was Margie. They quickly paused to enable her pick the call.

Margie couldn't wait for exchange of greetings to break the news she bore. She impatiently spoke up before Molly could say a word. "What!" Molly cataleptically exclaimed as she turned suspiciously to Lucas whose mood also changed instantly.

"What's the problem?" Lucas curiously asked as Margie hung up and she sluggishly shifted the phone from her left ear in sadness. "Mol, what is going on?" Lucas worriedly questioned again.

"Eric is dead," she sadly answered and staggered towards her bed. "Which of the Erics?" He inquisitively inquired again in confusion. "CEO of Miles Construction Company," Molly mumbled almost inaudibly.

"That can be true," Lucas hesitatively stated. "It is true, he is the guy my mom dated and Margie cannot make such expensive jokes." Molly emphatically chipped in with opened palms. "I spoke with him few minutes ago before heading to the Human Resource office to obtain your permit and he was fine," he quickly interrupted in bewilderment and added, "He is my closest cousin. He is Eric

Ferguson and I am Lucas Ferguson."

Lucas quickly took out his phone and called the closest police unit to Eric's residence. They reported that he was strangled to death and has been taken to the morgue. Instantly, Lucas in his tensed state stoutly concluded in perplexity. "Prisca is behind this. Probably, they had an issue…" then he held his forehead as he couldn't draw an evident suspect to his cousin's murder.

Molly sat tranquilly as he paced about the room trying to figure out what to do. Suddenly, he shouted, "Jamil!"

Molly quickly sat up as she understood he would be the next target. Lucas hurriedly rushed out as Jamil didn't pick his calls and Molly followed suit. They wandered round the estate but couldn't find him. Molly suggested that he should be checked at the point where they parted ways.

On getting there, they saw him from a considerable distance lying on the floor, faced down. The quick gaze they took at each other instilled great fear in them. They quickly rushed to him and pushed him over. Molly hastily made a random search on him for his phone as Lucas loudly beckoned on him.

Her heart beat increased to its highest rate as her right hand surfed through the videos. She impatiently clicked on one which she suspected to be the evidence as she scarcely concentrated on anyone.

Instantly, she breathed out in relief and assured Lucas that the evidence is intact. "Please call Karen and confirm your mom's safety," Lucas advised and Molly promptly took out her phone to make the call.

CHAPTER TWENTY ONE

The strategic confrontation

In a forth night, the government and research institute were already counting down to a successful cloning event. A new biological revolution awaits its manifestation. The shortlisted materials and resources needed for the cloning, had already been provided a week to the event. As Molly went through the materials to ensure all is perfect, Chokey, her cat and the giant tiger stumbled into her mind respectively.

She quickly rushed home for her when she realized that her mom's condition did not give her a chance to check on them. Immediately she entered the house, the dark sitting room instilled fear in her and she slowly traced the bulb's switch to where it is fixed and turned on the light. In relief, she carefully took a good look at the house. As her eyes went from the cushions to the television, kitchen and stairs, it also drew her back to her gruesome grief.

After a while, she summoned courage and climbed the stairs bearing in mind to grab the things she came for and leave immediately. While climbing, she sluggishly put her right hand into her bag, waggled her hand in it and brought out her phone. She suddenly stops at the door right before her to turn on her phone's torch. The torch portrayed the V-shaped light which illuminated the way to her room through the passage.

Suddenly, her phone hastily dropped into her bag as she held the door's handle and tried to open it, making the light that led her way go dim. In great panic, she swiftly deepened her hand into the bag and brought it out almost immediately.

She opened the door, found the wall switch with her torch and to her greatest surprise, they were all gone. "What!" She exclaimed astonishingly as her bag slipped from her fingers and dropped on the floor. Her mind wandered in confusion of where they could be. She quickly opened the restroom and peeped about but couldn't find them.

Then she walked up to the window and forcefully opened it, surprisingly, she saw Mario again after a long time. She unsurely thought of closing the window immediately but he already has his intent stares on her because the artless sound of the window attracted his attention.

"Hey, Mario," she greeted off the cuff with forceful smiles. "Hey!" he loudly replied with a full exhibition of his dentition as he transferred the hefty bag he carried to the other side.

"You are not done with this job?" Molly insensitively

asked in an audible tune, sticking out her head from the window. "Oh yeah at least it is better than your hopeless experiment," he retaliated smiling and Molly smiled back. He was insulting her and she knew it.

"Anyway, how was life in jail?" He questioned insolently in anticipation of her reply. "It was great," Molly replied happily.

"Really?" he retorted with utmost surprise. "Yeah," Molly replied as she lifted her body from the window's frame. "I met a young friend more sensible than you are," she added victoriously and slammed the window to his face.

She could still hear his vocal tantrums as she walked away from the window but she ignored it in search of things she considered of more importance to her. Abruptly, it hit her mind that she hadn't asked of Olivia since she left the jail.

After a while of thorough search for her pets alongside thought of how to reach Olivia, she bumped into them in the basement where Susan probably had dumped them but couldn't find her cat. She hastily guessed it must be somewhere in the neighborhood as she stepped out of the basement bearing the giant tiger and Chokey.

Molly took her time to clean up and package them. She stood for a while in the bus stop directly opposite her residence before a taxi came by. "This house will be rented in no time," she thought while nodding to the soft tunes from the car's radio with her lips inwardly clapped as the car drove off.

Few hours later, Margie happily rushed into Molly's office to break the most wonderful news she would want to hear."Oh my God!"She shouted with fear on entering the office prompting Molly to jump up from her seat. "What's the problem?

Why barge in like that?" She curiously asked in shock but got no reply then she walked up to the door to see what's after her.

She staked out her head and peeped through the door but found nothing. "What is going on?" she still asked kindly as Margie sat down. "For Christ's sake this is an office not a zoo, Molly"

Then Molly hissed heavily and shut the door behind her back. "I thought it's something serious," she sloppily replied as she took some strides back to her seat.

"Really," Margie chipped in as she turned and looked at her. "Come on, this represents what I do," Molly defensively stated.

They took a while to argue about Chokey's presence in the office. Molly won as she concluded that the giant tiger is hanging on her room's wall. If not it could have contributed to the zoo like setting of the office. While they took their

time to discuss, Margie broke the sudden news to her.

"I am pregnant," she whispered gently to Molly. Molly couldn't help but shout out joyfully. Her major gladness was that she is going to be a God-mother. They took their turns to declare what the unborn baby would answer. The gender obviously repelled amongst them as Margie chose female and Molly chose male concurring to Charles' choice. Molly ordered a pack of lemon flavored pizza and a bottle of vintage wine to depict the masculinity of the unborn child.

As they drank their wine sip after sip, Molly loudly declared with candid joy, "His name will be…" and stopped to think of something catchy and announced to Margie's surprise, "Ayo`la!"

"What?" Margie wondered with squeezed face of curiosity. "What's Ayola? Does that even exist?" She inquisitively asked amidst laughter. "No, no, no," Molly interrupted flipping her right index finger sideways in disapproval as soon as she dropped her glass of wine on her desk.

"It is Ayo`la, the O is a high one. Ayoooola!" Molly stressed while trying to express the tone intensity of the O. "Excuse me, what does that mean?" Margie still questioned with teasing gawks.

"It means… I don't know, but I guess *righteousness,*" Molly flippantly answered. "What!" Margie shouted and they burst into laughter.

"Origin please?" She still added while they laughed. "Some strange Greek word, I guess," Molly replied and they laughed harder.

"Trust me, that's weird," Margie assured as she tried to control her laughter. "I don't care. All I know is that, that's my God-son's name."

When their celebration died out, Margie suspiciously asked, "How's Lucas?"

"Lucas is fine, he should be here soon," Molly briefly answered and looked up to her while she said, "Ok" with conspicuous adjustments.

"You want to say something?" Molly unsatisfactorily inquired as she surfed through the books piled up on the right end of her table.

"Not really. But, what does he want?" Margie caringly asked this time with seriousness. "To be loved I guess," Molly haphazardly replied as she went through the books.

"Stop," Margie suddenly instructed as she held onto her fingers on noticing her careless mood and continued, "You think he should be given a chance?"

"Maybe," Molly answered after few seconds of silence. "You should be sure about this, Molly. You cannot remain in your shell with these weird creatures forever," Margie advised.

"Now that's offensive," Molly quickly pointed out but Margie's silence dragged down the severity of their discussion to her brain. "Fine," she sluggishly stressed. "I will give him a chance," she added as they smiled at each other having launched a beneficial plan.

"Prisca would be looking so pathetic presently in jail," Molly chipped in word after word in a crawly manner as she flipped her head sideways. "It is so unbelievable how my mom blindly trusted her," she added in disappointment as she looked Margie in the face.

"Friendship always has a string holding the two parties together. The reason for their commitment to each other can be so numb to the nearest stranger but they understand themselves that way. Just like us," Margie said pointing at Molly and to herself.

"We understand each other very well but our friendship is so off to others around. People do ask how I cope with you and your lifestyle but for me it isn't a big deal. In friendship, it is ordained naturally that one will be enduring or tolerating things more than the other, if not the friendship wouldn't work. So it was between your mom and Prisca," Margie explained extensively.

"Your mom endured a whole lot from Prisca which she overlooked for their friendship. She must have had Prisca's outburst because of Eric once or twice but she may have neglected it thinking that Prisca is harmless."

"At a point, I had to sound the warning to her but she didn't listen," she added throwing Molly into so much curiosity of when that happened.

"I paid her a visit while you were in jail because I couldn't accept it that a mother would be so cruel. I told her to be careful that Prisca might squeeze her head into her doom. Certainly, she didn't listen to me but I thank God it turned out this way except for Eric's case," Margie concluded as Molly was unquestionably short of words to utter. The only thing she held onto was her mother's safety.

Their gossips went on and on into Venomic Vanessa's state in the court. They tremendously mocked her self-assured speech on that day. They keenly demonstrated her flopped trials to reverse the judge's declaration while they laughed. They equally made absolute fun of the patches of disgrace plastered all over her face.

The best friend circus got into them that they almost forgot the setting is a work place. Their discussion and laughter grew in tones as their conversation dwindled from Smith's family (Tom, Dorcas and Shirley), to Ginika's professionalism, Picasso's sad demise; eventually, it boiled down to Olivia's welfare.

Shortly after much deliberation they scheduled a day to go and reunite the *Team MOM* again.

Lucas and Jamil entered in no time and embraced the lithe atmosphere already established in the office, but obviously missed the celebration which the ladies didn't care to unveil. The lads saw the bottle of wine and pizza but considered it none of their business and kept mute.

Lucas gave his newly found love a peck on her right cheek and suddenly stood still when she spoke up. "Margie, please meet my foremost and special cloning subjects," Molly introduced joyously with evident smiles.

"Wow!" Margie acclaimed as she took a quick look at them one after the other. "Really?" Lucas replied in wide arms of degradation. "That's amazing," Margie chipped in blissfully.

"Yeah, they willingly chose the F15 serum specimen," Molly announced to Margie's sudden confusion. "What does that mean?" she asked.

"My bad," Molly apologetically said amidst smiles. "The cloning specimen contains 15% of fox's serum. Every subject is allowed to choose speci…" she elaborated but was interrupted immediately.

"What! That's risky," Margie strangely declared. "Yeah, we considered that," Jamil quickly replied as he stood up from where he sat. "I mean it's just for thirty minutes and we will transform back to humans," he explained as Lucas affirmed his statement with nods. "Moreover, the Fox's serum is minute in the specimen."

"Fifteen percent is not minute, Jamil," Margie caringly stressed. "It is, compared the percentage of others. We considered all that, and the medical team assured its safe. So, we are good to go," Jamil still answered then shook hands with Lucas across the desk, paused for a while and

strongly added, "Although, my mother is against this but I will do it."

His mother's disapproval threw them into a shallow pit of silence for few seconds. "Hmm," Margie's audible out breath suddenly broke the silence. "I'm scared; this was the same enthusiasm Robin had."

"Relax, I am not Robin. I will pull through this. Besides, I'm not just the one taking it," Jamil assured and Margie breathed out heavily in submission holding unto the fervent assurance he gave.

Drawing conclusions from the way other districts in Gozax lives, one would conclude that Gozax's peace is intact. Literally, Maryland and recently Leach districts are going through fierce calamity. The Boatabs raided their homes and rendered it desolate, as they fled to Leach district for safety so did the Botabian army follow up against them.

"I will put an end to this once and for all," The President inaudibly declared as he stepped down from his car and walked towards the cloning tents set up at the army barracks in Kizimo district at the out skirts of Leach district.

The most recent update he received this morning increased his zeal to send the cloned soldiers against Boatabs.

The Boatabs had already camped at Leach District waiting for Gozax to attack. Unfortunately, what they expect wouldn't be what they will see. Previously, they have been taking the mantle of victory but it's about time they switch turns.

The soldiers and volunteers are all prepared for the task ahead. The intense training they have gotten on the behavioral changes one will encounter when cloned has strengthened their minds. The President and the Gozax Army Chief Commander cannot wait to record a triumph of ownership over Xylom limestone.

Molly and Lucas can be seen at one end of a tent inscribed C82. They took their time to chat and laugh as though it would be the last. In few minutes, Jamil stepped out of the same tent they stood by and joined them.

"Hey man!" He greeted as he widened his arms towards Lucas for a hug. "Hey!" Lucas replied as they wrapped their hands behind each other's back. Jamil equally hugged Molly.

"How do you feel? You don't seem nervous," Molly asked joyfully. "Nervous, I feel absolutely splendid, I really can't wait," Jamil answered smiling.

Their discussion lasted for a while then Jamil excused himself to say hello to a friend, leaving the other two.

"Surprisingly, Robin had this same eagerness as Jamil. Nobody could stop his brave decision to support the project," Molly sorrowfully said the moment Jamil stepped away from them but was suddenly interrupted by Lucas.

"I know where this is going," he quickly chipped in, held her hands and fixed his eyes on hers. "Jamil is not gonna die neither are my. Trash this negative feeling and focus on the positive results this is going to yield. Ok?"

"I really wish you won't do this. I will miss you," Molly tenderly acknowledged with affectionate facial expressions.

"I will miss you too," Lucas replied as he drew her closer to himself. "But, I will be back," he muscularly assured to lighten her mood. "You don't have to wait for too long, just call on me, Lucas! And I will be right there for you." They laughed.

An officer walked up to them while they laughed and informed Molly that she is needed at the control room.

"I will have to go now," she said immediately and held his hand tightly. "Alright, hang in there while I march out and get the job done," he answered with smiles. "And return," Molly asserted pointing her finger to his face to conclude the sentence. "Certainly," he affirmed amidst laughter.

Molly hugged him tightly like a depressed wife whispering sorrowful goodbye to a soldier's ear.

"See you soon," Molly whispered while they separated from each other. "You too," Lucas confirmed with encouraging smiles and then they took their time to lose hold of their fingers and finally did. He watched her keenly as she walked away. Obviously, he will miss her too.

The early morning of 9th September 2032, harbored an immense secret to most Gozax inhabitants and Boatabs entirely. The secret was tightly knotted to ensure it takes the enemy by surprise. The subjects were matched in squads of twenty each to their designated cubicles.

Totally, the data and analysis team recorded 250 squads, 255 medical teams, cloning 700 subjects and 700 foot soldiers ready to launch an attack. The stipulated order of dispatch is scheduled to be done such that 125 squads attack for 5minutes and return to rest while the other half takes the lead. Each attack session is scheduled for 5minutes interval.

Based on precise calculations, biological response to both internal and external stimuli starts in 30seconds which implies that if each pair of somatic cells takes 30seconds to lock up, the 13 pairs will take 390 seconds to lock up totally. Giving a total of 6minutes 30seconds.

The allowance of a minute given is to enable the clones turn back to humans within the last 90seconds of genetic lock up. Turnover of clones was

also planned to be done within the last 90seconds of attack.

The distance between Kizimo arm barracks and Leach is less than 4 kilometers which the clones were able to cover in a minute. Therefore, the clones have 4minutes to attack and return.

At exactly 3:45am, the army chief commander gave his reinforcement speech from the control room to kick off the event.

"Good morning amazing people of Gozax," he greeted as the subjects and the medical team members in the cloning tents responded immediately on hearing his voice over the speaker connected to televisions hung on the walls, and then he continued believing they responded.

"Today, we will out leash a new strategy in pursuit of what is rightfully ours. History will be made positively today. Our enemy has strongly camped on two districts of this city but we are going to march out this morning to their ruin. We have munched more than enough defeat, now is the time for the victorious sounds of our trumpet to drop," he addressed with vigorous movements of might.

"The Boatabs have just the army but we have more than that. We are going to see their heels as it runs off through Leach, Maryland and Xylom site. I summon you to go out there, fight like a Gozax patriot and return victorious," he spurred powerfully as the tent occupants retorted strongly in the ways they can. Instantly, he authorized the cloning to start.

Molly watched her dreams come true perfectly in dual process as the medical team in charge of each squad administered the specimen. In no time, the soldiers began transforming to animals of choice and were let out to launch an attack in batches. Each clone has a stop watch which regulated it. As the clones raced to their target the foot soldiers marched closely

with their gigantic weapons to launch an attack as soon as the clones retreat for a turn over.

Four kilometers away is certainly not too far for an army to detect relentless sounds of rigorously approaching foot stamps. The Boatabian watch dog quickly stood up and viewed the distance with his stethoscope from the height on which he stood but the intensive darkness instilled momentary blindness to his able eyes. He quickly notified his Chief Commander of the sudden terrific sounds approaching their camp.

"Set the war lamps above let's see what it looks like," the Commander authoritatively ordered over the phone. "Yes sir," the watch dog replied and speedily dropped the phone and loudly shouted, "Set the war lamps!"

Unfortunately, the clones were too close for a war lamp and preparation for a strategic defense. Shortly, after the lamps were released at about 2000meters above, one of the soldiers hopelessly declared, "Shit!" on sight of what was coming.

Their Commander desperately believed soldiers don't give up and ordered his army to fire. Sadly, it was too late for such moves.

Before they could assume their strategic formations, the clones stormed their camp and began attacking them furiously.

The Commander watched closely from afar with a stethoscope as they attacked. "Obviously, these are not humans," he thought as he slowly moves his stethoscope from one side to another.

"They have no guns nor bullet proofs but attacked with their jagged claws," he noticed while he still looked. "Their tireless approach was greatly evasive, the swift moves were too fast for an animal, the defensive tactics was incomprehensible, the bullets that hardly caught them

notified him of an impending doom. Just then he uttered aloud as he weakly slacked the hand with which he watched the fight, "Where did Gozax get these strange creatures?"

Instantly, he hopefully ordered for an immediate strategy they call "The Chameleon's time" which involves a mini retreat in order to hide in between structures available and strike.

Regrettably, Gozax army was out for more than that. Immediately, the clones retreated for a turn over, the foot soldiers speedily pounced on them before they could make a tangible move. Some of the soldiers were shot by bullets and many were killed by incessant drop of bombs.

The clones entered the tents one after the other, successfully changed to humans as they panted and sweated uncontrollably. Lucas hastily looked out for his friend as he panted and smiled on getting sight of him. A quick count of 500 clones that were released was made and unfortunately 10 soldiers were lost.

The Boatabian army kept drawing back as they fought with their last pack of might. The Gozax army kept on pushing because to overcome an army of more than 3000 soldiers isn't an easy task. With several clone turnovers and supplementation of foot soldiers they were able to push their enemy away from Maryland into Xylom.

Then the main war began. The Gozax army seemed too strong but equally made some loses of clones and foot soldiers. Molly would fearfully look into the camera that showed Lucas and Jamil's tent to ensure they returned with their batch.

The terrifying sounds of the bomb blasts and gunshots instilled great fear into Gozax's inhabitant such that not even a single soul stepped out of his or her house as at the time ticked 6am. In due time, the Gozax army discovered that their enemy reinforced their army from their city.

Then, the Gozax's Chief Army Commander contacted The Nuclear Science Research Center in Stockazul to break the Nizaro Bridge in Xylom which connected them with an intensive bomb blast. Gozax army's invading approach was immeasurable. Clearly, Gozax came fully prepared.

After so much trial to fight back with limited soldiers, it dawned on the Boatabian Chief Commander that he has lost the battle. He did think of a retreat because that would be a route less move and then he chose to hands up with his knees down to Gozax.

The tents were filled with victorious chants as they awaited the clones in the battle field to quickly return. Shortly, the victorious trumpets of Gozax began blowing after so many years. The people took to the streets in jubilation especially the inhabitants of Maryland and Leach district as the President of Boatab made the declaration of their surrender on television.

As the trumpets kept re-sounding, the clones rushed in one after the other. Shockingly, they weren't changing back to humans with ease.

Regrettably, the last batch to return was C82, Lucas and Jamil's batch. Suddenly, the tone of the music in the tents changed. Medical teams from other tents began rushing to help the intensified C82. Despite the lost count of 110 foot soldiers and 72 clones Gozax have at hand, 20 men were about to increase the record including Lucas and Jamil.

The arena was deepened into a horrific pot of fear of what would happen. Molly noticed there was trouble in her beloved's tent as she earlier felt, then she quickly rushed out to meet him but she was denied entrance into the tent.

"What is happening?" The Chief Army Commander desperately asked as he walked back to the control room with Molly, "Honestly, whatever I would say right now would be a guess," she replied with rapid breaths as they hurriedly stepped into the room.

Just then, the nurse who monitored their vital signs from a large flat screen computer suddenly declared with fear to the hearing of everyone, "Their blood pressure is dropping to the drastic points," her declaration was not meant to instill fear but to inform them of the severity of the situation at hand. Molly's major concern was for Lucas but the nurse's statement scared life out of her.

"Can I hear your thesis?" The Chief Army Commander requested by touching her to get her attention back. At that moment, Mr. Richard joined them to discuss what was actually wrong.

"I think the subjects have taken much of the specimen for a genetic unlock to happen with ease," Molly stated with shaking voice of nervousness. "Do you think it cannot be reversed?" The Commander asked while Mr. Richard kept mute and listened keenly.

"It will require much energy from the subjects and time. Sorry to say, in the case of a complete lock up, nothing can be done to reverse it," Molly lamentably revealed and the Commander wiped his bald head with his right hand in despair.

After a while, some of the soldiers miraculously began changing back to humans. It was instantly noticed that the blood pressure drops as any clone tries to change. Then Molly quickly advised for immediate infusion of normal saline as soon as they change to resuscitate energy they lost and enable them survive.

When 5 of the clones were remaining to change, Molly forcefully rushed into the tent and identified which was Lucas. She knelt desperately by his side as he lay lifelessly. She beckoned on him as he asked her to with tears forming streams in the deepened part of her neck.

Anybody presently who had witnessed Robin's case would understand the torture Molly was going through. "Lucas, please wake up," she miserably cried as she shook him uncontrollably. Robin's case was better because he had already turned to human but was lost during resuscitation but Lucas hadn't changed at all.

Her cry became loud when 2 clones among them took their time to change and Jamil was not among them. At this moment, her murkiness doubled. As Lucas's clone breathed harder so did Molly intensify her caring call on him, "Please come back," Molly quietly whispered to his ear.

Instantly, he jigged up to her shock. Her instantaneous laughter conjoined with the tears that dripped down her jaw. The medical team quickly took him from her for more medical attention. She hurriedly crawled to where Jamil's clone helplessly laid and began calling on him.

After several hours of calling and shouting to revive him, he still remained like a fox.

EPILOG

The Gozax army took Jamil's case up to ascertain if there is a window of revival. They took him for genetic screening to the best recommended places in the world but all to no avail. Several biologists did all can to initiate a change but their efforts flopped. The government is presently ready to do anything possible to see popular Jammy-Fox (as he is now called) in human form.

On the long run, Jamil had recorded reputable legacies to his name. The irreversible genetic lock up affected only his appearance, thereby making him look like a fox. Apparently, he can talk, laugh, eat, read and write like humans.

He joined the army, engaged in countless military trainings round the world, received behavioral adaptive trainings, fought for Gozax and handicapped nations in the globe and merited innumerable awards to himself. People fondly refer to him as Jammy-Fox, Talking Fox, and Military Fox, and so on to suit their reasons. Children instantly believed in the reality of cartoons when they encounter him in public.

He attended Lucas and Molly's wedding as one of the groom's men. He also took it upon himself to be the first to visit Molly in the hospital after child birth. How he hilariously lives his life baffles everyone. "My clone has never limited me to anything I determine to do," he stated in an interview on a global news channel. Presently, 2046 as dated the calendar, he is a senior Brigadier in the Gozax army.

Molly's ten years anniversary of launching her Animal-Human Cloning Center (AHCC) in Tokex was a success. She named her serum specimen after Robin and Jamil which she abbreviated as ROJAM cloning specimen.

Jamil received a mail as soon as he returned from the party. The mail summoned him for another exclusive genetic reverse. He hesitatively dropped his phone and sat on the sofa made especially for him. After a while, he suddenly ran through his stairs to the room where his entire awards are situated.

He sat down on the floor and took his time to stare at the evidence of the tireless effort he has made so far. After few minutes of staring, he rushed back to the sitting room and replied the mail saying, "I am comfortable the way I am."

The blogs and news channels took his decision round the world in a wink. "Jammy-Fox has solely decided to remain a fox," Lucas loudly read the newspaper's caption to Molly's hearing from the laundry room and they smiled at each other.

Robin made a sacrifice for family which eventually took his life forever.

Lucas, love saved him.

Jamil, the only son of his mother is literally stuck as an animal clone.